Little El

Little Elephant

W. J. CORBETT

Illustrated by Tony Ross

METHUEN CHILDREN'S BOOKS

British Library Cataloguing in Publication Data

Corbett, W. J.
The little elephant.
I. Title II. Ross, Tony 1938–
823.914 [J]

ISBN 0 416 17092 7

Contents

1

A Tragedy in the Clearing

Tumf was the luckiest young elephant in Africa. He had a mother who worried about him most of the time, a father who worried about him some of the time, and a circle of aunts who pandered to his every whim.

Tumf was also lucky in looks. He was as perfect as a young elephant could wish to be. His flapping ears were too large for his size, his trunk swept the ground when he walked, while his grey eyes were extra-small and squinty. As for his feet, they were of the enormous daisy-crushing kind. He also had the beginnings of tusks and was very proud of them.

But his luck didn't end there. Tumf also owned a drum. The drum was a gift from his adoring aunts. One day they had lumbered out of the sweltering jungle. The chief aunt carried a large, hollow log between her tusks.

'This is Tumffington's very own drum,' she said, setting down her burden in the centre of the clearing where the herd had made its home. She always called her nephew by his

correct name as she believed, 'Nicknames encouraged youngsters to get modern ideas and run wild.'

Tumf had been idly tapping a rock with the tip of his trunk, but at the word drum his squinty grey eyes glowed with interest.

'If Tumffington would like to come over and tap our present with his trunk he might be very surprised,' tempted the chief aunt.

Tumf rose from his stubby knees, raced across to the hollow log and, urged on by his smiling aunts, he dealt the log a mighty thump. 'Tumf,' replied the drum, mischievously speaking back his nickname. Delighted, Tumf rained down more blows. Tumf-ti-tumf-tumf.

From that time on, Tumf spent many happy hours bashing out tunes. But his aunts were always interrupting him. They nudged him and asked who he loved best in the world. It was such a difficult choice to make. Some days he loved his aunts best, other days his mother topped the list, then there was his father, who visited him once in a blue moon. Torn every which way, Tumf decided that, to be fair, he'd share out his love. One half he divided equally amongst his family, the other half he devoted to his drum. But his family wanted more.

'Tumffington is much too thin,' said the chief aunt, stuffing a bunch of bananas and a trunkful of green leaves down her nephew's willing throat.

'I think Tumf is getting much too fat,' protested his mother, squeezing into the circle of aunts to snatch the food from her son's mouth.

'He enjoys our diet, don't you, Tumffington?' said the chief aunt, tenderly tapping the youngster on the head as if he were a drum. 'Mother doesn't know what she's talking about, does she, dear?'

But Tumf kept his opinions to himself. He believed that everyone knew what was best for him. He never dreamed for a moment that he might be smug, pampered and spoiled. Dreaming his dreams and tapping out tunes on his drum, he never thought for a second that he might be an idle brat in need of a sharp lesson in life.

One day the aunts heard the sound of another drum, its evil rat-tatting beat out an onimous message, and sounded nearer every hour.

'The time has come for Tumffington to learn a new song on his drum,' said the chief aunt, her eyes sad.

'If Tumf must learn, teach him,' wept Tumf's mother, lumbering away. 'I just pray that he'll never need it.'

'Tumffington,' said the chief aunt, sternly, 'I want you to tap out a tumf-ti-tumf beat on your drum and let the words of our song burn into your brain so you'll never forget them. If anything should happen to you, these words could save your life.'

Puzzled but obedient, Tumf began to tap out his favourite rhythm with the tip of his trunk. He was very annoyed at his aunts for butting into his private life with their orders. But he loved them, too, and so he played his drum with all his skill and feeling. Taking up the tumf-ti-tumf beat, the aunts began to chant in time, their wrinkled faces disturbingly serious:

'Through the jungle, across the plain
Into the desert and out again
Into the river and out again
Through the swamp and out again
Round the bend and round again
Till your heart breaks once again.
Then . . .
Sniff through your trunk and flap back your ear
Now can you hear it ever so clear . . .?
Quicken your step and you'll safely come
To the tumf-ti-tumf of a drum.'

'Don't you care that your words might frighten him?' cried Mother from a distance. 'Anyway, the danger may pass us by if we hope a lot.'

'But it might not,' replied the grim-faced chief aunt. 'So, nephew, let's hear how much of the song you've remembered.'

Without a worry in the world, Tumf sang the

song word-perfectly, his trunk thumping vigorously on his drum.

'And don't ever forget a word,' warned the chief aunt. 'Are you listening, Tumffington?'

'Yes, Chief Aunt,' sighed Tumf. 'Now can I go down to the lake for my daily wash and brush-up?'

'Don't be cheeky,' snapped the elderly lady. 'And don't be late home. And don't forget to squirt lots of water behind your enormous ears. That is where the dirt collects.'

'Aren't I entitled to be in charge of my son's ears?' protested Tumf's mother. '*I* will warn him about the dangers of grime, if you don't mind.'

'But would he come back cleaner?' snorted the chief aunt. 'I doubt it. You've always been too lenient with young Tumffington.'

'I'm off to the lake now,' said Tumf.

'Remember to keep your eyes peeled for enemies,' the chief aunt warned. 'Take care that a whiskered mouse doesn't run up your overgrown trunk and cause havoc in your breathing passages.'

Tumf lumbered away, promising to obey all instructions to the letter. He usually shouted a cheery goodbye, but today he felt too irritated by his nice family.

'Where's my son Tumf?' demanded the huge bull elephant, his head and tusks crashing through the bushes that surrounded the clearing.

'You've just missed him,' replied the delighted aunts. 'What do you expect when you only come to visit him once in a blue moon? We think he's forgotten all about you.'

'So where's he gone?' asked Tumf's dad, ignoring the hurtful remark.

'Here, there, anywhere,' the chief aunt shrugged. 'And we don't know when he'll be back so don't ask. It could be an hour . . . a day . . . three days . . .'

'I'll wait, anyway,' said Tumf's angry dad. 'I'll wait here until the next blue moon if necessary. I've neglected him. But that is going to change – so I'm waiting. I'll see my son, come what may.'

But the aunts and mother and the herd ignored him as they always did. With lots of trumpeting and stomping they began to tear up trees and bushes by the roots as they set about improving the clearing. They soon vanished behind the curtain of dust they had stirred. It was as if a whole herd of elephants had suddenly ceased to exist . . .

It was the most delicious bathe Tumf had ever enjoyed. First he rolled in the sticky mud on the foreshore. Then, when he felt disgustingly dirty, he lumbered into the lake and crashed down on his side. For long minutes he wallowed blissfully. Regaining his over-sized feet, he promptly toppled over on his other side. Half-sunk, half-afloat, Tumf cocked a squinty grey eye at the sky and blessed his luck. Who would wish to be anyone other than a young elephant in a cold lake on a hot day with a talent for playing a drum when he was dry?

Heaving himself to his feet again, Tumf began his next bath-time ritual. Sucking up a trunkful of water he squirted it over his back in imitation of a tropical downpour. Then, filling up again, he tried to catch himself by surprise by flushing out his ears. He loved the roaring sounds that rang inside his head when he did that. Happy to be alive, he raised his soggy trunk to the blue sky and trumpeted loud and long, ignoring the angry pink flamingoes who were beginning to congregate and stalk in the water around him.

'Lakes are supposed to be quiet and calm,' they complained. 'How dare you come stirring up our bottom mud every day. Why can't you be less rumbustious? Better still, why don't you stay away from our lake altogether?'

'I am a young elephant and expected to be rumbustious,' said Tumf, indignantly. 'What gives you the right to try to calm me down? Anyway, this lake is as much mine as yours.'

'Let's remain friends by meeting half-way,' suggested a wise-looking bird. 'You be

14

rumbustious on the shore, we'll be calm in the water.'

'Done,' grinned Tumf, failing to spot the unfairness of the offer. 'I've finished my wash and brush-up, anyway. I was just about to wade ashore and sharpen my tusks on a rock.'

'What tusks?' giggled the flamingoes, peering close to see. 'You don't mean those two little nubs poking from your pouchy chops?'

'You won't say that the day after tomorrow,' Tumf shouted as he floundered ashore. 'By then my tusks will be as big as my dad's, who is coming to see me in the next blue moon. Then I'll come down to my lake and really stir you all up into a soup.'

Tumf's anger faded as he reached dry land. Suddenly he froze at the ominous beat of another drum echoing round the peaceful lake, sending the flamingoes flapping into the sky. The harsh beat was repeated again and again, rat-tat-tat-tat . . . then suddenly silence.

Tumf's large feet squashed and fidgeted in the sand, his trunk nervously swaying from side to side. The horrible sound seemed to be coming from his home. He didn't know what to do.

Then he saw a plume of blue smoke rising above the trees. His aunt's grim warning flashed through his mind. 'Don't ever forget one word of the song for it could save your life one day.' He tried to remember the words, but without his drum thumping along, the song was a mixed-up jumble. Suddenly, Tumf felt very much alone.

In a panic he began to race home, crashing aside the slim trees and bushes as he went. Breath rasping, knees buckling from the effort, he entered the clearing. His mother, his father, his aunts, the whole herd lay dead. Strewn about, their eyes stared glassily at nothing. Fresh blood still flowed from bullet wounds and from their jaws where their tusks had once sprouted. Tumf fell back on his haunches and

trumpeted his grief and despair. He began to blunder from this loved one to that, nudging them, trying to coax life back into their stiffening limbs. With his trunk in his mouth to comfort himself, he stood guard over his mother's body, willing her to stop playing this cruel game and return to life. Night descended but Tumf would not leave her. He refused to accept the terrible truth.

At dawn, blinded by tears, the little elephant began to run. He neither knew nor cared where. He just wanted to blot the horrors from his mind. He wanted to end his own life as quickly as possible. He ran for hours and only stopped when he crashed down on a carpet of thorns in a large and prickly bush. He closed his eyes, determined to die . . .

Seven days passed and Tumf was still alive but thin and wan. On the eighth day when the sun rose to reflect fresh light into the prickly bush, a watching bird, with more than a spark of compassion, decided to speak.

2
The Bald-Headed Veagle

'For the last time, pull yourself together, young elephant,' scolded the scruffy-headed bird. He was perched on a thorny branch above Tumf's slumped form. 'I insist that you open your eyes at once. Seven days I've been perched here worrying about you. Ignore me this time and I'll soar back to my mountains. I have my own noble life to live. My claws ache to clasp a crooked crag instead of this thorny twig. I yearn for the dizzy heights and the snow. So, for the last time, stir yourself, you self-pitying giver-upper. Just look at the state of you; all covered in fleas and flies and creepy-crawlies. Have you no self-respect?'

'Why should a noble eagle worry about my fading life?' murmured Tumf, drawing a deep breath and opening one bleary eye.

'Do I really look like an eagle?' said the bony bird, really pleased. 'That's probably because I am – or almost. In fact I'm a veagle, which is as close to an eagle as makes no difference. To strip me bare I'm an extremely noble, bald-headed veagle of the golden type, of course.

Some folk sneer that I'm a vulture with a snob complex. Yet how do you explain my love for sheer drops and snow? No, I must be a veagle with strong eagle leanings, don't you think? Anyway, that's my story and I'm sticking to it.'

'I don't care who or what you are,' said Tumf, listlessly. 'All I know is you are interrupting my death. Perhaps you really are a common vulture hanging around to pick at my bones. So rip and tear for all I care, life means nothing to me now that my mother is dead.'

'Doubting me already, eh?' replied the unkempt bird, moulting feathers all over Tumf as he bristled with annoyance. 'There's me trying to save your life and all I get are insults. Come on, little elephant layabout, let's have you up on those great daisy-crushing plates of meat. Let's have you stomping about to get the old pins and needles going. Then when the blood is whooshing through your brain again you can explain to me why you are trying to commit suicide when your life has barely begun. In the meantime, I'll sing you a romantic ballad to cheer you up. At the very least, my song will drive the flies away.'

So on that eighth morning of dying, Tumf staggered from the prickly bush to begin a new life. His grief was still a sharp pain but he obeyed the bird and began to do some gentle, unstiffening exercises in the sun. Meanwhile, the veagle launched his cracked voice into a

ballad that sent the flies scooting away in clouds from Tumf's parched and wrinkled hide.

'O you lofty mountains tall
In your crags the veagles call
Wheeling swiftly through the air
Keen eyes darting everywhere . . .
Gazing down through steely eyes
Yes, the veagle rules the skies
When the darkness breaks the day
Then at last he soars away . . .'

'What do you think of the ballad?' asked the bird, warily eyeing Tumf doing his knee-bends.

'It certainly drove the flies away,' said Tumf, beginning to perk up. 'And it has a very nice beat . . .' but as he spoke he slumped to the red earth and wept.

'There, there, little troubled one,' soothed the veagle, flapping down from his perch. 'Tell me your name, my very first friend, so that I may treasure you more.'

'Tumf,' snuffled Tumf. 'My name is Tumf.'

'Short for Tumffington, no doubt,' said the veagle, gently. 'Well, never be ashamed of who you really are, or you'll end up like me.'

'Yes, veagle,' said Tumf, gratefully. 'I don't care at all that you are a vulture pretending to be someone above his station.'

'Now, now, just because we're getting our

humour back,' chided the grinning bird. Then he was all serious. 'But tell me, why should a lovely young elephant wish to end his life in a thorny bush? Let your Uncle Veagle share the burden.'

Tumf blurted out his terrible story . . .

'What, everyone, down to the very last aunt?' gasped the outraged veagle. 'And all for the price of their tusks? I weep for our Africa, I truly do. We must do something to stop this . . .'

'And then I ran and ran until I stumbled into the thorny bush to die, when the next thing I remember I was being ordered to pull myself together by a noble veagle.'

'Yes, well, I've always tried to be noble,' preened the bird. 'But now, I'm interested to learn more about your song, especially if it can save *this* elephant.'

Tumf sadly shook his head. 'I can't sing it without my drum tumfing along; the words would come out in the wrong order. And my drum lies silent in the clearing with my dead family.'

'So we need a drum,' mused the veagle. 'A makeshift drum. A good-natured drum that won't mind being beaten a little.'

Flapping down from the bush he began to strut up and down, his beady eyes scanning the surrounding grassy clumps and ferny dells. Suddenly, he gave a triumphant cry: 'Behold our new drum, young Tumf. Slow-moving and mild-mannered, perfect. Now then, prepare to holler, "Hey you, come over here," at the top of your voice. Our drum should plod over here in about half an hour.'

'What kind of drum has legs to plod on?' asked Tumf, confused.

'You'll see,' said the veagle, his vulture-like wattle wobbling as he chuckled. 'Are you ready to holler?'

'Quite ready, veagle,' Tumf replied, nervously clearing his throat, and very curious.

'Then let it rip,' yelled the bird, filling his moulting chest with a huge lungful of air.

'Hey *you*, come over here,' bellowed the friends.

3

The Drum who made Speeches

'Are you shouting at me or chewing a brick?' called back the drum, his beaky nose poking through the ferns, his eyes wide with astonishment. The drum was in fact a tortoise.

'Well, there's nobody else, that's for sure,' retorted the bird. 'Who would want to live with you? Anyway, we aren't in the habit of chewing bricks. In fact we're chewing over whether we should include you in something very important. But if that's your attitude we'll move on and find someone less flippant.'

'Why should you want to include me in something important? I'm just a nobody tortoise with a talent for making speeches that nobody, not even the trees, listens to. So, why am I suddenly being canvassed to do something important? By complete strangers too?'

'Because you look the important type,' smarmed the bird. 'How would you like to be vital in our scheme of things?'

'*Me . . . vital?* Vitally famous?' cried the tortoise, his head in a delicious spin. 'It's what

I've dreamed of all my life. Well, can you beat that?'

'We are hoping to beat you, actually,' answered the veagle, honestly. 'How do you fancy becoming a drum?'

'You mean you want me for a non-speaking role?' said the disappointed tortoise. 'For how long? I don't want to be a drum for the rest of my life. I've always yearned to be a rabble-rouser and tour Africa shouting my mouth off about all the problems that plague our lovely continent. Can you guarantee that I'll be allowed to spout the odd speech while serving as a drum?'

'You'll be allowed all the free speech you want,' promised the veagle. 'Especially after you've served your purpose as a drum and we chuck you out on your ear. Then you can devote the rest of your life to plodding round Africa shooting your big mouth off. Perhaps you can save the elephants?'

Tumf looked very sad.

'That sounds generous enough,' whooped the joyful tortoise. 'Don't move an inch. Before I dash across to join you I have a few bitter words to say to these sneering trees who've ignored me all my life.'

As quickly as it had appeared, his beaky nose withdrew. Moments later they heard a very sad song, weepily delivered in a high and reedy voice. Yet there was a note of triumph in the tone and the trees seemed to sigh with regret.

'Who will you snub now
Tall waving trees
After this song when the ferns fall dumb?
Who will you mock now
Tall waving trees
While I'm running away to become a drum?'

'That's told 'em,' shouted the tortoise, his injured pride healed at last. 'Goodbye, weeping trees, I'm about to make dust towards my new destiny. You won't have poor old tortoise to kick around any more.'

'Which means that we can relax for an hour,' sighed the veagle to Tumf. 'Tortoises make marvellous drums, but they're terrible sprinters. So what shall we talk about while we're waiting?'

'I think I've got a fly in my eye,' said Tumf, his squinty left eye screwing up in pain.

'Yes, well, time-passing chat was never stimulating,' murmured the veagle, his hooded eyes closing to snatch an hour's rest.

It was a pity that Tumf blinked at that moment. It was a pity that the veagle closed both eyes at that moment. They missed the astonishing sight of the liberated tortoise scorching across the one hundred metres of red earth that separated them. The young elephant had barely opened his eye to blink again before the tortoise arrived in a blur of speed and a cloud of red dust. Dumbfounded, Tumf and the veagle stared down at their new drum, who was grinning up at them, his breath healthily even.

'I've always kept myself in tip-top condition in case something turned up,' he said, proudly. 'I've spent my life jogging up and down behind those ferns. At one time I had the whole of my family jogging up and down with me in the hope that something would turn up for us all. But sadly, last year, my wife and little ones jogged away from me in the dead of night. The day before they left they wept that they didn't know what they hated more – the jogging or my speeches. Alas, I was too busy composing a speech to see the writing on the wall. And so I was left alone to talk to the trees, who also hated my one hundred and twelve carefully crafted speeches. Thank heaven I've memorised every one. So, with my potted history off my chest, I wish you both a cheery hello and thank you for, from what you say, I'm at last into something vitally good.'

'You've memorised one hundred and twelve speeches?' gasped Tumf. 'Where does your brain store them all, especially the long and boring ones?'

'My speeches are not long and boring,' bristled the tortoise. His clawed foot reached up and over as he tapped the top of his shell in annoyance. 'I'll have you know that every one of my speeches will go down in history as a cracker. I'll spout you one as an example:

'My fellow Africans,

'I am squatting high above you on this hot rock to bring to your attention a very important matter in a speech entitled:

'"Should we get Hot Under the Collar in the Face of Global Warming?"'

'Before you get too heated I should remind you that you're here to be a drum,' interrupted the veagle. 'It's your musical abilities we're interested in. This half-dead little elephant has recently lost every member of his family to ivory poachers. We're here to help him remember the words of a song that must hold the key to his future.'

'Oh, you poor thing,' soothed the shocked tortoise, gently scratching the tip of Tumf's trunk with his clawed paw. 'If it's any comfort I've composed a speech with elephants in mind. It's entitled: "Why are Living Elephants worth less than their Dead Tusks?" and I'll be driving that message home when I begin my rabble-rousing tour.'

'You'll be driven back behind those ferns if you don't button your beaky lip,' snapped the veagle. 'Me and young Tumf are fed up with your speeches already.'

'Just listen to the bird with a bee in his bonnet,' mocked the tortoise. 'Don't worry, baldy, I've got you taped in a speech as well.

It's entitled: "Why do Vultures pose as Eagles by calling themselves Veagles?" Would you like to hear some more?'

'I would,' said Tumf.

'Well, I wouldn't,' said the veagle. 'Now, can we get on and talk about why me and my friend need you for a drum?'

'Intrigue me,' was the reply.

The bird explained. 'In Tumf's head is a song that his aunts taught him. The trouble is, he can't sing the words in the right order without the tumf-ti-tumf-tumf of a drum to keep his mind on track. Do you follow?'

'Now I understand,' said the tortoise, nodding. 'Just suggest the beat and I'll drum the whole of Africa awake.' He cocked an eager paw over the top of his shell, his rear paw poised to pound out the counter-time.

'If you could play tumf-ti-tumf-tumf over and over again, it would be just right,' said Tumf, hesitantly. 'At least I think so.'

'Like this?' shouted the veagle. He began to stomp around in a circle, his bony wings jerking rhythmically as he muttered, 'Tumf-ti-tumf-tumf,' beneath his breath.

'Almost exactly like that,' cried Tumf, excitedly.

'Or would it be more like this?' yelled the tortoise, vying for attention as his front paw whacked his shell and his rear one thwacked the red earth in perfect counter-time.

'Exactly like that, tortoise,' cried Tumf, his trunk beginning to sway from side to side in delighted harmony.

'Let's make music then,' called the puffing veagle. 'Come on, young Tumf, sing out loud and clear.'

At last Tumf could sing the words in perfect order. He saw in his mind's eye the lovely faces of his dead family and he wept as he sang:

'Through the jungle, across the plain
Into the desert and out again
Into the river and out again
Through the swamp and out again
Round the bend and round again
Till your heart breaks once again
Then . . .
Sniff through your trunk and flap back your ear
Now can you hear it ever so clear . . .?
Quicken your step and you'll safely come
To the tumf-ti-tumf-tumf of a drum.'

'I reckon the song is a journey across a map,' said the tortoise, 'and waiting at the end of that journey is a new home and a new drum for our precious charge. Let's up-sticks and go at once.'

'You are brave, tortoise,' said Tumf, admiringly. Then his creasy face fell. 'But I'm a very unworldly elephant. I feel I'm much too small to tackle the journey through my aunts' song. I always had them to look after me.' And, unable to say any more, Tumf popped his trunk into his mouth to comfort himself.

'With me in charge you have nothing to fear, my darling,' chucked the tortoise. 'Instead of aunts you've got Uncle Tortoise now.'

'Who's Uncle Tortoise?' demanded the angry veagle. 'I'll have you know that I've been Tumf's Uncle Veagle for much longer than you've known him. Anyway, as Tumf's first and best friend I say that I should be in charge of our expedition. The song mentioned nothing about a tortoise with the gift of the gab being in charge.'

'Nor did it mention a balding vulture who fancies himself an eagle,' asserted the tortoise, spiritedly.

'Please don't argue,' wept Tumf. 'My aunts and mother used to argue over me and if you keep fighting I'll make the journey alone. I will, even if I don't arrive . . .'

'Now see what you've done to my adopted son,' shouted the tortoise, glaring at the veagle.

'You started it,' huffed the bird. 'Anyway, I have first claim on Tumf's trust.'

'You mean you once did,' puffed the tortoise. 'Until he found out what a phoney you are.'

'Stop!' cried Tumf. 'I am going to find a route through the map of the song on my own.

Goodbye to you both. One day you may stumble across my bones in some lonely place but that is a long tomorrow away.' So saying, he heaved himself on to his enormous, daisy-crushing feet and shambled weakly away into the jungle. He was soon swallowed up by the darkness, his trunk in his mouth, his tab of a tail miserably tucked between his unsteady legs.

'I refuse to say goodbye to you, my Tumf,' cried the distraught veagle. 'I refuse to let you travel alone without me shouting the way ahead.'

'I'll never allow my first and best friend to blunder over Africa without a drum as a loyal companion,' yelled the tortoise. 'I love him more than even my best speech could say.'

'You can't love Tumf more than I do,' bristled the veagle. 'Everyone knows that love has to grow, and I've known him longer than you have.'

'My love might be shorter, but it's deeper than yours,' flared the tortoise, squaring up to the angry bird.

Meantime, wobbling weakly on his still jelly-like legs, Tumf blundered into a snarl of sneaky creepers just inside the dark-green jungle. Trumpeting his fear, he fell in a tangled sprawl. At once, the flapping veagle and the sprinting tortoise were hurrying to fuss around him. But they managed to quarrel over who

was the leader of their party rather than help Tumf.

'I know I'm unworldly, and still wet behind the ears,' Tumf said, wincing with pain as he tried to break free of the creeper, 'but it's my song, and my map, and I won't have you two falling out every step of the way across it. Promise me that, veagle, tortoise.'

'You'll never hear a cross word from me again,' promised the bird. 'I'm yours to command, my Tumf.'

'From this time on I'll be your sweet-tempered drum, my best friend,' vowed the tortoise.

'Then together, in harmony, we'll set off through the jungle for the plain,' cried Tumf. 'And if we survive the hardships, it will be because we pulled together as a loving team.'

'You're right, Tumf,' said the veagle, nodding more feathers from his nearly-bald head. 'And I'm glad to say that I'm beginning to feel a deep affection for our tortoise. I can't wait to start pulling at him – I mean with him.'

'I've just realised what a lovely bird our veagle is,' said the tortoise, his slitty eyes moistening at the corners. 'I shall miss him when he flies off to scout the way ahead. I just pray that he doesn't crash into a tree while he's doing his eagle impressions.'

'Best foot forward then,' cried Tumf, delighted. 'Except for you, of course, veagle.

You'll be eager to launch yourself into the air. Don't forget to zip back and inform us if danger threatens.'

'Or just drop in like a stone,' smirked the tortoise. 'And by the way, after the jungle comes the plain. If you plan on scouting it you'll find that it's a flat, green thing with lots of wind moaning over it.'

'I know what a plain looks like,' snapped the veagle. Then his voice softened as he spoke to Tumf, busy flexing his wasted muscles. 'Good travelling through the jungle, little one. Your way ahead will be safe with me.' He strutted off to find an open space to take off from. After three tip-over-tail botched attempts he finally became airborne. After two near-fatal crashes into the tree-tops he managed to gain enough height to wobble out of sight.

'And now for your role, tortoise,' said Tumf, gazing through his squinty grey eyes at his makeshift drum. 'When we begin our march through the jungle I'd be grateful if you bring up the rear. I'd be much obliged if you keep glancing over your shoulder and if you see a lion padding along drum a single "tumf-ti-tumf-tumf" danger signal on your shell. If you spot something even more dangerous, I'd be relieved if you drum a double danger signal as loud as you can.'

'What is more dangerous than a prowling lion?' asked the puzzled drummer. Then his beaky face crinkled into an incredulous smile. 'You don't believe that old myth about cheeky mice scampering up elephants' trunks to cause sneezing fits?'

'My aunts always warned me to be cautious,' said Tumf, feeling a bit silly, then defensive. 'My chief aunt was the wisest of the wise. She often said that the greatest dangers are the small ones you barely notice.'

'Your chief aunt must have been beautifully prim and proper,' said the tortoise with a twinkle. 'I'll bet she fumed if anyone called you Tumf. I'll bet she always called you something posh like your proper name, for instance.'

'What proper name?' said Tumf, stiffening.

'Like "Tumffington",' grinned the tortoise.

'It always made me squirm to be called by my whole name,' answered Tumf, sadly. How he wished he could still hear his chief aunt's haughty voice.

'Be glad she named you out of love. You'll always be slangy "Tumf" to me. So what now, Tumffington-Tumf, I hear Africa calling.'

'Then let Africa hear our reply,' cried Tumf, the itch to travel nagging at his daisy-crushing toes. I am going to travel through the jungle at a very fast pace. I know you're a good sprinter, but can you keep it up for miles and miles?'

'I'll be worrying at your heels every step of the way,' shouted the tortoise. 'And don't spare a worry for padding lions and

mischievous mice. If they dare to attack I'll jolt
them back with speeches to shame them for the
rest of their lives.'

As for the veagle, Tumf could not have
wished for a more dedicated scout. Though he
kidded himself that he had the binocular vision
of an eagle, he was definitely short-sighted.
But he did his best, dangerously clipping the
leaves from the trees as he blindly scouted the
way ahead for his beloved Tumf.

Africa barely stirred a leaf from its slumber as
the determined band of brothers became
swallowed up by the jungle. It just watched
and waited, enticing them in. To calm their
fears, the little elephant and the tortoise sang
the song of the aunts as they hurried along the
snaking path that led to the plain.

4

He's not Heavy he's my Brother

The jungle was stickily hot and deluged with bursts of pelting rain. Creepy-crawlies of every shape and hue stopped, stalked and flitted about their mysterious business. The trail was slippery with rotting leaves and mosses and Tumf often stumbled. Snakes slithered and slipped across their progress, hissing from cover as the travellers passed by. Frequently, bands of curious monkeys swung down from the heights and derided the brothers with many rude gestures. It was when Tumf lumbered beneath a nut tree that the kidnapping occurred. Clinging to its lower branch was a small, sad-eyed monkey. Tumf dislodged the tiny creature, who fell in a flurry of arms and legs on to the elephant's broad back, where the rocking motion quickly sent him off to sleep. Tumf was so anxious to leave the creepy jungle that his passenger went unnoticed by him or the tortoise, busy frightening off impudent mice.

Then, at last, the dark-green jungle began to thin out and became shot with light. Suddenly

Tumf and the tortoise were emerging on to a green and rolling plain, stretching as far as the eye could see. Grateful to be in the sunshine, Tumf and the tortoise noticed that the veagle had landed and was waiting for them. He looked hot and bothered and appeared to have lost a lot more feathers. In fact while trying to soar like an eagle he had been attacked by the genuine article, who had tried to carry him home to his mountain fastness in time for tea. Somehow the terrified veagle had torn himself free. He was now determined to keep the humiliating experience to himself.

'How did the scouting go, veagle?' asked Tumf, slumping gratefully down in the long green grass for a rest. 'Did you spy any dangers we should try to avoid?'

'Not a one.' He forced a smile. 'You'll be glad to know that this plain only stretches to the next horizon. Hardly more than a half-day journey.'

'Oh good!' whooped Tumf. 'I hope you're going to say that there are lots of pools dotting the plain, I'm dying for a nice wallow. This journey through a song is turning out to be a doddle. We'll soon be sunbathing through the desert at this rate. I've always loved the sun. After the sticky jungle, it will be like heaven.'

'Actually it's that sandy playground that worries me,' said the veagle. 'From the air it seems to stretch on for ever, with no sign of ending. And I must warn you, Tumf, I saw not a drop of water in that golden hell.'

'It's only a large beach,' cried Tumf, confidently. 'I'm beginning to feel we've reached the end of our journey already, apart from the tiniest hiccup that we'll easily overcome. All we need to do is keep up our spirits and enjoy ourselves along the way.'

'I'm quite prepared to keep my spirits up,' said the bird, suddenly angry. He was glaring at the tortoise who was squatting at Tumf's heel, chewing on a green salad he'd rustled up. 'But that drum is definitely going to dash our spirits if he doesn't pack up singing that mournful dirge. Must he sing sad songs and cheerfully chew at the same time? I don't think he's taking this journey seriously enough, Tumf. I suggest we banish him behind his ferns where he belongs.'

'Who's singing?' flared the tortoise, choking on his greens. 'Chewing I am, but singing I'm not.'

'Then who is singing? I can hear it too,' asked Tumf, his enormous ears flapping like radar dishes. 'What is this song without a singer?'

'I think it's beginning to explain itself,' said the veagle, hopping close to peer up at Tumf's back. 'The singing is coming from the furry brown lump you've grown on your back. You've developed what we wise veagles call a musical back. Perhaps if we stay very quiet and try to make out what it's singing about?'

Tumf peered fearfully over his shoulder, his squinty grey eyes confirmed that he had a hump on his back all right. But his ears confirmed that it was a smashing singer as it sang in a wistful and dreamy style:

'Sometimes I dream I am rolling away
Rolling away from my mum and dad
Sometimes I dream they don't want me to stay . . .
How is it I don't feel sad?

Sometimes I dream I am stolen away
Stolen away from my mum and dad
Sometimes I dream they had prayed for this day . . .
How is it I don't feel bad?

Sometimes I dream I am not worth a nut
Worth not a nut to my mum and dad
Sometimes I dream they have slammed their love shut . . .
How is it I feel quite glad?'

Suddenly, the hump on Tumf's back began to stir, tiny knuckles rubbing at sleepy eyes. It was a little brown monkey with a blue nose. The hitchhiker gazed around in wide-eyed surprise.

'Has my dream ended?' he said. 'And if it

has, where am I, and who are you?'

'We're not part of your dream,' snapped the veagle. 'This is a real-life drama you're interrupting. So why are you lounging on our Tumf's back? Hop down and swing back into your jungle at once!'

'I'm swinging nowhere,' retorted the tiny monkey, cheekily. 'You gang of ruffians have stolen me away from my mum and dad, which means that you'll have to face the consequences. Mind you, my dad hated me anyway. He was always saying that he couldn't stand another minute of my cheek. In fact, he's waiting to thrash me within an inch of my life for pinching an extra nut last supper-time.'

'A common hitchhiker and thief wishing to join our band of brothers?' gasped the outraged veagle. 'I've never heard such cheek.'

'I'll get even more cheeky the more we get to know each other,' the monkey insisted.

'Do you realise that you've been scrounging a lift on the back of a young elephant who's only recently lost every member of his family to poachers?' raged the bird. 'We three aren't out for a stroll. We are setting out across a map through a song to find a new drum for him. The last person we want to join our band of brothers is you.'

'Please, veagle,' interrupted Tumf, taking a shine to the cheeky hump on his back. 'I didn't mind him hitching a ride at all. But I do see a

problem. He is much too young and small to travel all over Africa with us. I do think he should return to his parents, and thank his lucky star that he still has them.'

'You can talk,' said the monkey, cheekily. 'From here I can see that your ears are still soaking wet. You've no right to tell me what to do. You're only a suck-pap yourself. In my opinion, your so-called friends are using you.'

'Monstrous lies,' cried the veagle.

'Cut out my heart,' blasted the tortoise.

'Don't be a spoiler as well as a thief,' Tumf chided the cheeky monkey, gently. 'You've no right to speak about my loyal friends in that way.'

'I know,' wept the tiny monkey. 'I've always been too cheeky to cope with. And too greedy. When Dad ordered us brothers and sisters to take two nuts each, I had to pinch an extra one. I know Dad will track me down to thrash me within an inch of my life. That's why I'm desperate to go with you.'

'That's settled it,' said Tumf, all misty-eyed. 'Veagle, tortoise, I think we should invite this cheeky monkey to join our band. I think his dad is cruel.'

'Band?' said the monkey, his brown eyes sparkling. 'Can I play the drum? I've always wanted to play the drum in a band.'

'No, you can't,' snapped the tortoise, jealously. 'I do all the drumming around here.'

'I'm not always cheeky,' the monkey protested. 'Even my dad said that I'm an engaging little chap when I'm being honest.'

'You'll have to curb your cheeky ways if you want to join our band of brothers. We don't insult each other in this group. Our motto is one for all, and all for one,' warned Tumf.

'Fair enough,' agreed the monkey. Then his round, brown eyes sparkled again. 'So, if it's one for all, and all for one, who's the one prepared to gather me three nice nuts for my supper? Only, according to my body-clock, it's close to sunset and I like my supper on time. Then afterwards I like to fall asleep in my own arms. Who feels like going scrumping in the jungle?'

'Forage for your own nuts,' shouted the fuming veagle. 'And you'd better hurry about it.'

'You really are a cheeky little monkey,' chided Tumf, smiling. 'But wait a moment.'

Rising to his feet he turned and lumbered back to the edge of the jungle. With his long and delicate trunk he cropped a large bunch of bananas, then he began to stuff them into his mouth until only three remained. With a chuckle he offered these over his shoulder. With a dart and a snatch the tiny monkey was soon licking his lips after a satisfying supper. Moments later he was curled and wrapped in his own arms on Tumf's broad back, dreaming

46

and singing in his sleep the same wistful song as before.

The sun was poised to set when the band of brothers set off across the plain towards the fearsome desert. Their voices were strong and firm as they drummed the song. After all, they had conquered the jungle.

'Scouting, scouting, taking off now . . .' yelled the veagle.

'Demanding to play the drum indeed!' fumed the tortoise, sprinting along on Tumf's daisy-crushing heels.

'Be charitable, tortoise,' said Tumf, gently. 'I know the cheeky monkey is irritating, but he's suffering from a parent problem just like me.'

'But you lost your parents to the poachers, Tumf,' protested the tortoise.

'It is the same,' insisted Tumf, a tear squeezing from the corner of his squinty grey eye. 'His parents may still be alive, but they're lost to him. Don't worry about him being a burden on our backs. He's not heavy. He's my brother for ever and a day.'

The tortoise had to agree.

Across the dark and shadow-chased land the pair lumbered and sprinted. The journey was flat and tedious, and the friends passed the time exploring their private thoughts. The little elephant's mind cast back to a time when every happiness was his, when he had been the focus of so much love. Now that love was gone, and all he had in the world was a song and loyal friends. A lot to be thankful for, but Tumf quietly wept as he rolled across the plain before the setting sun and remembered.

Sprinting along behind him, the tortoise was also consumed by dreams. His main one was to see Tumf's problems solved and then he would set the rest of his own life into famous motion. In his head he had the speeches, out there in Africa were the waiting audiences.

Across the plain cruised the veagle, doubtless dreaming his own dreams of greatness.

And on Tumf's back snoozed and dreamed a tiny monkey. But his dream was a nightmare in vivid colour of his angry dad.

As the tortoise nipped along behind Tumf, his eyes alert for danger, he was suddenly struck by the beautiful sight of the sun setting over his friend's sail-like ears. Later, as the moon rose, he was dazzled to watch it riding majestically between those ears. Only one incident marred the uneventful march: a mischievous mouse bravely dashed from cover to sneak up Tumf's trunk for a wheeze. Betrayed by the bright moonlight, the tiny creature cowered as the tortoise sprinted forward to tick him off in a long speech, entitled: 'Why the Whiskered African Mouse should be Severely Curtailed when he Gets Above Himself.'

Then the tortoise attacked the stars and the moon with words that caused them to blink and hide themselves behind cloud. But all too quickly a new sun was rising behind Tumf's swinging rump, a terrible sun, a sun that would threaten to destroy the confidence and the unity of the close-knit band of brothers.

5

Through
the Golden
Nightmare

The sun was spitting down from its midday height as the travellers passed over from the plain to the beginning of the desert. Even the most ambitious heart began to wilt as eyes stared out into that awful cauldron of waste and heat.

The veagle had landed again. He was waiting, his toes as hot as burning twigs as he hopped from foot to foot on the fiery sand.

'Tumf, I have to report that this desert seems to stretch on for ever. After a whole night's scouting I saw no sign of the river. And there's something else. During my flight I saw nothing but piles of whitening bones littering the sands. I think they are a warning to us to proceed no further.'

'Please don't persuade us to turn back, veagle,' cried Tumf. 'I don't want to go back to the prickly bush to die. What's happened to the Uncle Veagle who fired me with the will to live again? Where's your old spirit, my friend?'

'It's sunk a bit,' the bird admitted, ashamed.

'I'd urge us onwards through the desert if my shell wasn't almost red-hot,' said the tortoise, his usual cheerfulness long evaporated. 'If it's this hot merely on the edge of the desert, what will it be like in the middle? Perhaps we should turn back and search for a route around the desert instead of through it?'

'Tne tortoise and I are in perfect agreement for once,' said the veagle. 'Let's backtrack around the golden nightmare. And Tumf, I must press the point, we'll find no water to drink if we attempt this folly.'

'Perhaps you are both right,' wavered Tumf. 'Perhaps we should turn back.'

On Tumf's back the tiny monkey shook a

scornful paw at the trio as he began to sing a scathing song:

'Fly back to your dreams where the eagles cry
Sprint home to your ferns where the bored trees sigh
Trudge back to the bush where you hoped to die
But this brother means to go on . . .'

'Don't be so quick to disgrace us,' said Tumf, peering over his shoulder. 'You'd never cross the desert on your own. You'd be lost without extra nuts to eat and water to drink.'

'I'll cross the sands somehow,' said the monkey, his paws clenching and unclenching with worry. 'Last night I dreamed that my dad was hot on my trail, and I saw my mum sitting sadly in the fork of her favourite tree, not lifting a paw to defend me. I'm dead anyway. At the end of my terrible dream my dad's face appeared in close-up to warn me, "I'll follow you to the end of the earth, and to the end of time to see that you get your just deserts," and he wasn't talking about nuts.'

'Just pray that your dad gets to you before I do,' muttered the pacing veagle.

'If I could just once grasp that cheeky monkey's nose in my jaws,' sighed the tortoise. 'But alas, he never comes within range.'

The monkey buried his crumpled face into his paws and began to weep piteously but he was also peeking through his splayed fingers to note how Tumf was reacting. His cunning was rewarded.

'I won't have this little mite threatened,' warned Tumf. 'Whatever his faults, the cheeky monkey is a full member of our band of brothers and is entitled to his opinions and dreams. And in a way he is right. We are behaving like cowards. So, veagle and tortoise, shall we slink back to the safety of the plain or shall we forge ahead through the desert as laid down in my aunt's song?'

'Call me insane, but OK,' shrugged the bird, his heart sinking into the pads of his blistering feet.

'Who'd try to stop a small but determined tank?' replied the tortoise. He winced. 'But first aid first, eh?' Stretching his beaky nose over his shoulder he began to huff and puff on his shell to cool it down.

'Forward then, band of brothers,' cried Tumf. Raising his trunk in the air he blasted a defiant trumpet at the shimmering, menacing desert ahead.

'Into the jaws of death,' yelled the excited monkey, clinging tightly to Tumf's neck as the little elephant moved off across the scorching sand. 'And may my dad praise me as a hero one day, instead of a son in need of a good thrashing.'

'Ever onward,' shouted the tortoise,

sprinting to catch up with Tumf's rocking and rolling motion.

'Into the air once more,' puffed the veagle as he took off once again, ' . . . to pinpoint the river that I may have failed to spot on my first sortie.'

'And which you'll probably fail to spot again,' shouted the tortoise.

More in faith than hope the veagle flew out across the desert to search for the river beyond the sands. How glorious to feel the air rushing through his hot toes and balding feathers. But just as the searing sun began to slide into late afternoon he flew beak-first into a sandstorm. Dashed by furious winds, his eyes stung by whipping sand, he just managed to beat back to the others. He landed in an exhausted sprawl, barely managing to croak out a warning before the sandstorm hit them all full-force.

Falling on to his side, the terrified little elephant had the presence of mind to reach his trunk backwards and sweep the squealing little monkey into the protective tent of his outsize ears. And there they lay quaking as the howling winds dumped tons of sand on them. The tortoise withdrew all his vunerable parts into his sturdy shell and crouched at the tip of Tumf's tail and rehearsed new speeches as he waited for the storm to blow out. The veagle, bruised and battered, managed to scrape out a pitiful refuge beneath Tumf's fat belly. All around and everywhere, the sandstorm continued to wreak its fury and havoc.

The stillness and silence that followed the passing of the storm were eerie. Stars glittered in a clear sky. After the heat of the day the night was cool. Parched with thirst and aching with cramps, the brothers emerged to face the world again.

'It must be a good luck omen to have survived such a terrible storm,' cried Tumf, rivers of sand spilling from his back as he rose to his feet. 'Now I'm more convinced than ever that we'll reach the river. We'll soon be quenching our thirst in lovely blue water.'

'My throat is as dry as a parrot's,' croaked the monkey, swallowing hard. 'But it's caused by fear as well as thirst. I'm certain that my dad is lurking out there amongst the dunes.'

'All the more reason why we should start travelling again,' said Tumf, 'if the veagle and the tortoise agree.'

'I think it would be wise,' said the tortoise, looking worried. 'Travelling by night is much easier than travelling by day.'

'What about you, veagle?' asked Tumf. 'I'd value your wise experience very much.'

All eyes focussed on the bird, who had been strangely silent for some time. To Tumf's distress he looked a picture of listless and balding misery. He was standing apart from his

friends, his back turned to them as he stared out across the desert at nothing much. Now he began to shout harshly and bitterly, 'What use am I any more? Just leave me here to die. Go on without me, I'll only be a burden to you.'

'You, a burden, veagle?' said Tumf, shocked. 'As if you could be. Why do you talk like this? We know how much you have suffered but your strength will return. Turn round, look us in the eye and see for yourself how much we still believe in you.'

'What's the point in turning round when I don't know where you are?' replied the bird, brokenly. 'Are you standing to the left or the right of me?'

'Right behind you, actually,' said Tumf, his fears mounting. 'Just swivel one half circle on your claws, and there we'll be.'

Looking more like a cold robot than a warm bird the veagle shuffled around in the sand to face them. His eyes had been so sandblasted by the storm that he was now quite blind.

'Oh, my poor friend,' mourned Tumf, stroking the veagle's bald head with the tip of his trunk. 'If you could only see our tears.'

'And to think I was so cheeky,' sobbed the tiny monkey. 'If only his eyes could flash anger at me.'

'Don't pity me,' said the bird. 'Get on with your journey through the song. Go by the orange star hanging low on the horizon, I feel the river will flow just beyond it, As for me, I plan to take a long walk quite soon, and I may be late returning.'

'Nonsense,' scoffed the tortoise. 'This band of brothers will stick together come what may. Anyway, your condition is not all that serious. You've just got a bad case of sand in the eye, nothing that a good dollop of water won't cure. So stop moaning. Come on, everyone, let's follow the orange star and track down the river.'

'But how will our blind bird travel?' asked Tumf. 'He can't fly, can he?'

'Well, he's not riding up here with me,' shuddered the monkey. 'Even sightless he could do terrible things to the likes of little me.'

'The problem is solved,' grinned the tortoise. 'Though there's no love lost between us, I'm prepared to offer him the end of my tail. He is welcome to grip it with his beak and be led by me so long as he doesn't mind having sand kicked in his face.'

'Be sensible, veagle,' cried Tumf as the bird staggered blindly away. 'Please come back, we need you.'

The veagle reluctantly allowed himself to be guided into his new travelling position by Tumf's gentle trunk. They set off by the light of the winking stars instead of a hateful, burning sun. In the lead ambled the little elephant, the tiny monkey clinging to his back and chattering as he pointed a skinny arm at the low-hanging, orange star ahead. Close on Tumf's heels sprinted the tortoise, smiling his beaky smile each time he accidentally kicked sand into the veagle's face. But in fairness he did stop to reattach him when the bird became unshackled.

Tumf's nightmare began in the ghostly hour before dawn. Trudging up and down the endless dunes, he saw heaps of white bones littering the way rise up and come to life. There was malice in their voices: 'Where were you when your family were being slaughtered in the clearing, precious Tumffington? Why did you linger down by the lake? Why didn't you run straight home when you heard the terrible drum? Why are you still alive while your loved ones lie rotting in the clearing?'

'I didn't understand what was happening. How could I have known?'

'Perhaps you didn't want to know,' argued the sneering bones.

'That's not true, I needed time to think.'

'Only a coward hesitates,' spat the voices. 'Tell the truth. You shut your ears to the sounds of danger to save your own miserable skin.'

'You lie. I am not a coward,' wept Tumf. 'I would have given my own life to save my family if I'd arrived home in time.'

'Excuses. If you are so eager to die, then die here in the desert.'

'Away, wicked demons,' interrupted a gentle and familiar voice and, instantly, the evil bones fell lifeless in the sand.

'Chief aunt!' Tumf stumbled in the sand as he dashed to her. 'Are you really alive? Where have you come from, where is my mother?'

'I come from the calming side of your dreams, my Tumffington,' answered the beautiful wraith. Her trunk reached out wistfully to caress the little elephant but worlds divided them, although her comforting voice continued: 'Battle on and finish your journey to the end of the song, little one. Tackle each danger no matter how hard the road may be. I know you will, you are amongst the bravest of the brave. Trust in your friends, and be of good heart, my Tumffington. Morning approaches and soon you will wake to new challenges. Goodbye, love of my stolen life, remember my words. I am very proud of you. You used to be a little spoiled but you're not now. Remember we love you.'

'Wait, chief aunt,' implored Tumf.

But her bones fell back into the sand and she was gone with the rising of the sun. As its strong light began to sweep across the desert the monkey and the tortoise were alarmed to see Tumf pawing at a heap of bones in the sand, weeping.

'My chief aunt was here. She spoke to me . . . but now she's gone.' His squinty grey eyes poured tears into the sand.

'Come now, my sad young friend,' said the tortoise, gently. 'We are all beginning to suffer from the heat and thirst. The desert does strange things to travellers. Sometimes they see mirages of things that aren't really there.'

'It was no mirage,' shivered the tiny monkey. 'My knees feel like jelly after all the running I've done. I can still hear my dad's threats ringing in my ears as he chased me round and round the desert.'

The poor, blind veagle sighed long and deep. 'I also had a strange experience in the hour before dawn. I imagined I left my body and soared up into the high mountains of eternal ice and snow. But now everything's gone dark again.'

'That's it, I've heard enough,' shouted the frightened tortoise. 'The sooner we get out of this desert the better. It's clear that you're all cracking up. Our future depends on me hanging on to my own sanity. I'll be issuing the orders from now on. It's obvious that you three are too potty to think for yourselves.'

'Who's potty?' flared Tumf. 'We three don't much care for the tone of your voice, tortoise.'

'OK, so you think you are sane,' the tortoise sighed. 'Let's put it to the test.' He sprinted up the nearest dune, dragging the blind bird behind him. Mystified, Tumf, with the monkey on his back, climbed to stand beside them.

'Well, what do you see?' asked the tortoise, waving his clawed paw at the bleak sameness of sand stretching in every direction.

'I see a huge, blue sparkling lake,' said a delighted Tumf. 'And around it I can see groves of banana trees and is that my mother trunking the bananas down for me?'

'I see a stream babbling over rocks,' interrupted the monkey, licking his dry lips.

'And I can see nut trees loaded down with millions of extra nuts.'

The blind veagle raised his beak to savour the aroma. 'I can smell an icy, mountain brook chock-full of trout and salmon. Excuse me while I go and catch a succulent fish for my supper.'

'Now do you see what I mean?' cried the tortoise, restraining the veagle. 'You're all suffering from desert-pottiness, so I'm taking charge before we all die. The things you see, you don't see at all. What your aching eyes can't see are the crowds down there cheering my speeches and chanting, "We love you, tortoise." Of course you can't, because you've all gone potty.'

'Well, if we are potty and you aren't, you'd better take charge, tortoise,' said Tumf, his head whirling with heat, his throat rasping with thirst. 'But I can't understand why you won't let me go down to the lake to bathe.'

Ignoring the crowds who were baying for another wise speech the tortoise led his friends down the dune and up the next.

There were three further days of hell. Every upward slope of every dune promised to reveal the river. But the dunes rolled on in endless, dry profusion. And the low-hanging orange star seemed to remain as far away as ever. But the tortoise refused to give up and fought his own thirst and pottiness, his tail sore from the beak of the blind veagle, who clung like grim death to the end of it.

Then on the fourth day, as the sun rose hotter than ever, the heart of the tortoise gave out. Half-way up the highest sand dune of all he collapsed in a fit of dry weeping. He just wanted to die. But one stubborn spark of grit remained. He raised his head to peer blearily up the dune. Near the top he could see a pink and green snake lazily sunning itself half-in, half-out of its burrow. Groaning in pain the tortoise heaved himself to his clawed paws and clambered upwards to hurl himself at the surprised sunbather and gripped the snake's throat firmly between his beaky jaws.

'Ouch, me neck,' protested the snake, trying to wriggle free. 'What happened to friendly niceness between strangers?'

'I lost all my niceness three days ago,' gritted the tortoise from the side of his clenched mouth. 'So just listen, my "nice" little friend. Just co-operate and you'll be all right, refuse and I'll bite your head clean off. Now then, I demand that you tell me where the river is. And if you know what's good for you it'd better be no further than a short mile away. So give me good news, or start praying.'

'But how can I help with my breath in a vice?' gurgled the snake 'Why can't you be nice and release my throat, then we can talk like nice civilised folk?'

The tortoise slightly relaxed his death-grip. 'Can you promise me that the river is less than a short mile away? Because if you can't my friends below are going to die an awful death in your desert, and I'll blame you. Your life hangs on your reply.'

'The river is nothing like a short mile away, I regret to say,' gasped the snake.

The spark of grit began to shrivel in the tortoise's heart. But it began to pound fast again as the nice snake explained.

'The river flows by just the other side of this dune,' he said, then added, defensively, 'I can't help it if the river is closer than you hoped. I hope you're not going to take your anger out on me.'

On the contrary, the tortoise could have kissed the snake. 'The river lies just over the crest of this dune,' he shouted, happily. 'Why didn't you say so in the first place? And I'm sorry about your neck!'

'So am I.' The nice snake winced. 'But you did demand that the river should be further away than it really is and I've never told a nasty lie in my life. I was brought up very nicely, you see. If you are staying in this vicinity for a while you'll learn how perfectly mannered I am.'

'I'm sure you are, bless your little pink and green body,' whooped the tortoise, chucking the nice snake under his triangular chin. 'But I've too much to do at the moment. I've got to tell my band of brothers that we are saved.'

'But you've only seen my top half,' said the nice snake, his yellow eyes dancing with excitement. 'What if you discovered that my lower half was even prettier? You'd be astonished, eh?'

'Can I express my astonishment later,' pleaded the tortoise. 'I really must dash, if you'll excuse me, nice snake.'

'I excuse nice folk anything,' called the snake as the tortoise rolled and scrambled back down the dune. 'After you and your friends have visited the river, perhaps you'd all like to come back and express your astonishment when you see my lower half? Then I'll sing you a song. A very nice song full of colour and perfect manners, I might add . . .'

But the tortoise was gone.

'Get up on your feet, my gallant band of brothers,' he cried. 'One final effort and we'll be splashing about in all the water we crave.'

Hope swelled in Tumf's weakly beating heart. With a tremendous effort he regained his aching feet. With the monkey hauling tug-of-war style on his trunk he managed to plod those few more steps, the tortoise and the staggering veagle bringing up the rear. Panting for breath, the little elephant gazed down on the most delicious sight he had ever seen. Rolling and gushing below was the blue river, its wavelets dashing at rocks in surges of white spray.

'Excuse me, but hello,' said a nice, polite voice from close at hand. 'You might think that I'm a pink and green snake with exquisite manners, but you'd only be half-right. So when you've all enjoyed your wash-and-brush-up I'd be delighted to show you something truly astonishing. By the way, I hope you like singing for I've a song I'd like you to hear. But I'm interrupting your bathing. Please forgive me. I'll see you later then?'

But Tumf and his friends were too far gone and too desperate for water to heed the snake, however polite. They had to rejoice that the golden nightmare was over.

6
Flashes of Bright Blue

Raising his tired trunk in the air, Tumf bellowed a trumpet of gladness. Then curling himself up into an enormous ball he rolled tip over top down the dune to land with a mighty splash in the river. There he began to drink as many millions of gallons as his belly could hold. The monkey came rolling down the slope, too, in a flurry of arms and legs. After giving the blind veagle a nudge up his tail-feathers to topple him riverwards, the tortoise flipped over on his back and tobagganed into the water in streamlined style.

Never had plain old water felt so good. Soon the little elephant was squirting trunkfuls over the squealing monkey and the gravely paddling tortoise. As the veagle came hurtling down the dune in a cloud of moulting feathers and terrified squawks, he was quickly seized. Tenderly his friends bathed his swollen and sand-caked eyes until, to the joy of them all, he cried that he could see again.

Then, thoroughly soaked through and bursting with water, the brothers went their

different ways to rustle up well-deserved meals. The cheeky monkey quickly discovered a nut tree. Stuffing two in his mouth he looked guiltily around before gobbling down a third. Wandering along the bank, the little elephant blundered into a bush bearing his favourite flavour of leaves. A few minutes later only the stump of the bush remained. In the meantime, the tortoise was tucking into a bed of watercress, making loud slurping noises as he chewed and rehearsed his speeches at the same time.

As for the red-eyed veagle, he went fishing. Standing in the shallows of the river he waited, crooked beak poised, for an unwary fish to swim by. One did, and was quickly speared and swallowed. He was so absorbed with filling his empty belly that he failed to notice he was being watched. Strung out along an overhanging branch were a family of kingfishers, Mum, Dad, and their three jostling chicks. The parent birds were angry, the youngsters shuffling uneasily. The dad bird suddenly plucked up his courage and, fluffing up his brilliant blue feathers, he uttered a warning:

'I hope you know you're trespassing? We kingfishers have sole fishing rights along this stretch of river. How dare you steal the fish from the mouths of my youngsters. Anyway, I always thought that vultures preferred to rip and tear at rotting carrion? So why pinch fish from hungry chicks?'

'Because I like fish,' snapped the veagle, whirling around to face the nervous family. 'Anyway, who says I'm a vulture? In fact I'm a veagle, which is completely different. Don't you recognise one?'

'We recognise a poacher when we see one,' said the dad bird, bravely. 'And as the legal fisherfolk in this area, we demand that you make yourself scarce.'

'Or you'll make me, I suppose?' challenged the angry veagle.

Sensing that there might be a fight, the three chicks edged along the branch, away from their angry dad who was glaring eyeball to eyeball with the veagle. The chicks longed to fight but they knew they were too small. They also knew that their brave dad was nowhere near big enough, which was why their mum was weeping.

'Your size doesn't frighten me, you baldy thief.'

Fortunately the veagle heard Tumf hailing him from the other side of the river and turned back. Boasting that his threats had sent the veagle packing, the kingfisher puffed himself up, feeling like a king indeed.

A high-spirited celebration was in progress as the bird arrived. The tortoise, his beak-mouth stuffed full with dripping watercress,

71

stood planted on the shore, his foot tapping an enthusiastic tumf-ti-tumf-tumf on his shell. Nearby, Tumf and the cheeky monkey were performing a clumsy jig as they lustily sang the words of the song that had brought them so far:

'Through the jungle, across the plain
Into the desert and out again
Into the river and out again . . .'

'Don't get too carried away, young Tumf,' said the veagle, damping their high spirits. He was his old bossy self now his sight was restored. 'Don't forget we have to cross the dangerous swamp next. And the sooner we tackle it the better. So let's travel.'

'Can't we stay here a bit longer?' pleaded Tumf. 'Can't we stay here by the river and regain our full fitness before we brave the swamp?'

'I agree with Tumf, you old spoilsport,' glowered the tortoise. 'The whole of Africa is waiting to hear my speeches, but I'm going to polish off that watercress bed before I leave. So pipe down, baldy.'

'I agree with the veagle,' said the monkey, glancing nervously up the dune. 'There's someone slinking and sliding about up there. What's the betting it's my dad come to settle accounts with me?'

'Don't be a silly monkey,' chided Tumf. 'It's probably just the wind stirring the sand.'

A nice voice was heard: 'If I might interrupt, a while ago a tortoise promised that he would return to express his astonishment. Well, I'm sad to say that he hasn't yet. Why is he ignoring me? Why are you all ignoring me? I hope you aren't turning out to be less nice than I thought. Notice how nicely mannered I am, even though I'm very annoyed.'

'That's not my dad,' said the monkey, thankfully. 'My dad was born without a nice bone in his body.'

'I know who it is,' sighed the tortoise. 'It's the pink and green snake who pointed the way to the river. He's come for his pound of flesh or its equal in praise.'

'Didn't I save your lives?' cried the snake, reproachfully. 'Why are you leaving so soon? Aren't you interested in being astonished by something? Don't you think I'm nice enough to pass the time with?'

'You must be nice to save our lives,' said Tumf, his kind heart softening. 'Thank you very much. By the way, I like pink and green. They are my favourite colours.'

'Hold on,' cried the excited snake. 'You haven't seen my lower half yet. But first I'll blow your minds with an astonishing song.'

'Must we listen to this bore?' groaned the tortoise.

But his protest cut no ice with the nice snake who began to sing the song he'd been dying to sing for ages:

'I'm glad you think I'm very nice
But nice alone will not suffice
For have I got a treat for you . . .
I'm nicer half-way down.

I'm glad I'm nice in pink and green
But nicer still is nicer seen
For have I got great news for you . . .
MY TAIL IS LUMINOUS BLUE.'

The nice snake then whipped his pink and green body around in a flurry of coils to expose his tail. Beautiful up top he certainly was, but downstairs he was truly breathtaking. His tail was bluer than the river. Bluer than the balmiest of summer skies. Even bluer than the bright plumage of the kingfishers. But it was the glowing quality of his tail that made him unique amongst snakes. It shone as if lit by some energy within. Wiggling it in the air, the snake eagerly waited for a reaction. He was disappointed when the veagle brought him down to earth.

'Very impressive,' the bird snapped up the dune. 'Now if you've quite finished making an exhibition of yourself, perhaps you will slide back into your desert and let us get on with our business. We are following a map through a song that will lead to a new drum for this orphaned little elephant. So get on your way, you slithery show-off.'

'Won't!' shouted the defiant snake, forgetting his manners. 'I want to become a brother in your band. I'm fed up with having this astonishing tail with nobody to gasp at it. I want to travel and show it off to everyone. Anyway, my luminous tail will come in very useful when you travel through the dark, smelly swamp. And you'll have my nice company and cheerfulness to perk you up when you get down in the dumps. So here I

come!' With that, he began to slither zig-zag down the dune, his luminous tail waving in the air like a beacon.

'I'm not keen on snakes, nice or not,' shuddered the monkey, leaping on Tumf's back. 'I think our little elephant should tramp with me up the dune and crush him. And if my dad is lurking up there, we can squash his head at the same time. Sort of kill two snakes with one bird . . .'

'No, we don't,' said Tumf, frowning. 'This band of brothers will harm nobody.'

'We can't afford to be squeamish, Tumf,' said the tortoise, snapping his beaky jaws. 'Do you want to be burdened with a snake who's too nice for comfort? Shall I sprint up the dune and finish what I started? I'll have his head clean off with one bite. Or give him such a ticking-off speech that he'll turn tail and flee? Take your choice, Tumf, for I love you too much to fall out.'

'I won't have the nice snake harmed,' said Tumf, sharply. 'And yet, at the same time, I know that he'll never fit in with us. Make him realise that, tortoise, but be gentle.'

In a flash the drum of many words was sprinting up the dune to bar the way of the gorgeous snake.

'Now look here, nice-stuff,' he warned, pushing his beaky nose against the snake's triangular one. 'When I say shove off, I mean shove off. Get the message?'

'Won't,' cried the nice snake, dissolving in tears. 'Why can't I come with you? I'd be as loyal a brother as anyone.'

'He refuses to turn back, and for your sake, Tumf, I can't use violence,' shouted the tortoise down the dune. 'So shall I threaten him with a speech entitled: "Why should Nice Snakes be Treated Leniently just because they're Nice?"'

'I think we should ignore him,' said the irritated veagle. 'Let's get on with our journey and hope we can shake him off if he follows us.'

'You'll never shake me off,' shouted the snake. 'I'll join you if it kills me. I must belong

77

to something worthwhile, otherwise I'll be driven mad by loneliness.'

'I agree with the veagle,' said the nervous monkey. 'I'll only be happy when we've left all frightening things behind us.'

'You've heard what my friends think,' called Tumf. 'I wouldn't mind your joining us but you must admit that you're a bit too small and polite to take part in a venture as dangerous as ours. For your own good I suggest you wriggle back into the desert. After all, that dreadful place has little enough niceness as it is.'

'Won't,' yelled the snake, advancing down the dune again. The tortoise shrugged and sprinted to rejoin the brothers.

'On your own silly head be it then,' Tumf sighed. 'But if you become hopelessly lost, you'll have only yourself to blame.'

'I'll take my chances,' said the snake, defiantly. 'But you'll need the likes of little me and my astonishing tail before you get through the swamp.'

'Oh, shut up,' snapped the veagle. He turned to his friends. 'So are we travelling, or are we not?'

'I hope we're doing the honourable thing,' said Tumf, turning around to wade across the river. 'That nice little snake deserves much more than his lonely life in the desert.'

He was too ashamed to glance back at the little snake. And so they continued their journey through the song. As they waded across the river and into the trees, it became stinkingly clear that their plough through the swamp would be no picnic.

The nice snake was confident that he would catch up with the brothers when the terrible swamp forced them to a snail's pace. Then he would come to their rescue. With his luminous tail held proudly aloft he entered the pitch-black swamp, prepared nicely and politely to solve and save and, into the bargain, notch up all the praise he believed he deserved.

7

A Very Nasty Swamp Varmint

'I can't see, I'm drowning, tortoise,' cried Tumf as he slipped and stumbled amongst the rotting roots of the mangrove trees. 'Can you hear me? Are you still there? Is the cheeky monkey still safe on my back?'

'We're still here, Tumf,' gasped the tortoise, swimming through the putrid ooze to grasp his friend's flapping ear in his beaky jaws. 'Don't worry, the monkey has taken to the trees. But I won't desert you. Just hang on and obey my tugs on your ear, we'll soon find safer ground.'

The awful darkness and the terror of drowning in the sea of filthy mud had knocked out all the little elephant's confidence, his trunk was tucked into his mouth again. The tortoise led him by his ear to a small island of higher, drier ground. Just before he hauled himself ashore, Tumf felt an excruciating pain shoot through his rear foot. Trumpeting in fear he blundered ashore and collapsed, while the outraged tortoise stood guard. The tiny monkey conquered his own fears to come and comfort Tumf. The veagle appeared, like a bat

on the back of a black night, folding his wings to perch beside Tumf's injured foot. He had good news for the brothers. He had glimpsed the mountains beyond the swamp and a twisty path that wound upwards towards the pass that opened on to pastures new. But all he could think of was Tumf's foot. The heel was bloody and torn and beginning to swell alarmingly. The veagle and the tortoise and the cheeky monkey stood guard over the little elephant. If danger came, they would be ready.

Suddenly, they heard a voice, hard and completely without pity. It chanted an evil song, sniggering and giggling as it spat out the words:

'I love to make travellers wrinkle their noses
I love to smell high from my ears to my toeses
I giggle to nastily savage a heel
For varmints love hate with a zeal.

I love to make visitors fall in my trapses
I love to cause pain when my yellow teeth snapses
I snigger to viciously tear out bright eyes
For varmints love life with despise.'

Cackling and joyful splashing followed and seemed to be approaching the small island.

'What do you want from us, varmint?' cried the veagle, his bony knees knocking as he stared into the gloom. 'Why did you savage our young Tumf who's done you no harm? Why do you hate all of us who've done you no harm? The little elephant is only a poor orphan in search of a new drum. And we are only his loyal friends who are helping him find it. So let us pass through your swamp without further violence, I beseech you. Be kind and guide us through this awful maze to the bendy mountains beyond, for I'm sure that beneath your gruff manner you're really quite reasonable.'

'Wanna bet?' screamed a blood-curdling voice from the darkness.

'That's definitely my dad,' shivered the monkey.

'I'se a'coming to sort you out,' yelled the terrible voice, sounding even nearer. 'Guess who'll be sorry when I arrive?'

'If only I had a speech to make a varmint feel ashamed,' said the tortoise, racking his brain for ideas. 'What does a swamp varmint look like when he's at home?'

'Get ready to find out,' bellowed the frightful voice only metres away. 'Start shivering and shaking to view a varmint in all his merciless glory. And prepare to have lots of fun. I hope you lot love quiz games because that's what we're going to play when I arrive.'

'Refuse to play with the tyrant,' cried the injured Tumf. 'Tell the vicious varmint that we're not in the mood for games. Tell him that if I were fit he'd feel the end of my trunk across his gloating face.'

'Oh, so our hero fancies another ankle bit to the bone?' bawled the varmint, sounding like a loud loudspeaker now. 'Someone should warn him to curb his tongue. Unless he don't want to take part in our quiz show?'

'This is no time to be noble, Tumf,' hissed the veagle from the side of his beak. 'Let's humour him. I suspect we'll never get out of this swamp if we don't. The varmint sounds like he'd resort to torture if he didn't get his own way.'

'You'd better believe it,' sniggered a voice from behind a rotting log. 'I always torture quiz contestants who get their answers wrong. They receive my special Booby Prizes. For instance, if a vulture gave me the wrong answer to a question I'd tear out the rest of his feathers, and knot his legs behind his neck. If a cheeky monkey was stumped for an answer I'd stuff him with nuts and scoff him for supper. As for a tortoise who talked too much, I'd turn him upside down until he stewed in his own juices, to be enjoyed as a hotpot. Nor would a little elephant get off scot-free if he got his answers wrong. His bitter Booby Prize would be to have three ankles gnawed to the bone to match his fourth. Of course, miracles can happen. If someone just happened to get their quiz question right, they would win my Top Prize. Their reward would be the freedom of leaving the swamp, with yours truly leading the way. But that's never happened. I hate giving away my Top Prize.'

'You gruesome, unfeeling varmint,' cried Tumf, struggling to his three good feet and, unusually for him, spitting out harsh words. 'Isn't there a chink of compassion in your soul? Show yourself, fiend! Let's see what the lowest of the low looks like, if you dare!'

The mysterious varmint was happy to oblige. The ooze around the shore of the small island began to churn and bubble. The brothers had expected to be frightened out of their wits. But in the dim moonlight the varmint appeared more comical than anything. His tiny head was topped by a mop of silver, mud-slicked fur. His whiskers were luxuriant and drooping. Shining through his whiskers jutted two huge buckteeth that seemed to be grinning, but probably were not. Across his fat belly were folded two paddle-like paws that twirled in a constant state of impatience. All these strange features were wrapped around in a thick blanket of more silver fur that steamed and stunk to high heaven. Even Tumf stifled a giggle. But the eyes of the swamp varmint were no laughing matter. They were huge and slanted downwards into slits, and glowed a cold emerald green through thickets of silver

lashes and filled with tears as he raged.

'Don't talk to me about chinks of light, especially not blue chinks which remind me of when I was little, when I once saw the sky. But the leaves of the mangrove trees blotted it out. They grow more leaves than they need to keep me in the dark where they can keep an eye on me. I'd love to see the sky just once more in my life, but because I can't I take my anger out on travellers by torturing them to death. Are you lot ready to be tortured to death? After the quiz show, of course.'

'No, we are not,' said the veagle, trying to control his trembling. 'Why should we have to pay with our lives, just because you can't gaze at a chink of blue sky?'

'Why don't you paddle out of the swamp into the light?' asked the puzzled tortoise. 'The sky is always outside, waiting.'

'Because I love black stinking mud,' replied the mixed-up varmint. 'I hate anything clean. I'm happy when I'm crawling with rotten worms and putrid crabs. Now then, are you ready for the quiz?'

'How about if we get our answers right?' said the indignant little elephant, his painful foot forgotten for the moment.

'Then you win the Top Bonus Prize,' the varmint replied, rubbing his paddled paws over his belly, 'which is a free passage through my swamp with me as your guide. But you can forget it, nobody gets out of here alive. Now then, quiz question number one is for you: "What is the most terrible sight you've ever seen?"'

'The most terrible sight I've ever seen was my family lying dead in the clearing,' grieved Tumf.

'Wrong,' cried the delighted varmint. 'The most terrible sight you've ever seen is me, don't deny it. Look forward to your Bitter Booby Prize when I return to gnaw the rest of your ankles. The next question is for the almost bald vulture-bird. Question: "What is the most glorious thing you've ever seen?"'

'The most glorious thing I've ever seen was myself in a dream, wafting over a range of snowy mountains,' replied the dreaming veagle.

'Wrong, wrong,' bellowed the varmint, his webbed paws hugging his fat belly in glee, his emerald eyes sparkling. 'The most glorious thing you've ever seen is a swamp varmint rising from the mud in all his majesty. Your Bitter Booby Prize will be to be the rest of your feathers plucked out and stuffed down your throat. But you'll have to wait for your prize until I've dealt with these others.'

'I expect the next wrong answer will be mine,' said the miserable monkey as the varmint's lovely green eyes scrutinised him.

The varmint thought deep and long. Then his fearful, comic face lit up with an idea. 'I know, answer me this: "Who is the greatest thief in past and living memory?"'

'I am,' admitted the monkey, bowing his tiny head. 'Because every time my mum gave me two nuts for tea, I'd pinch a third to make it three.'

'Wrong, wrong, wrong,' yelled the gleeful varmint. 'I'm the greatest thief of all. Haven't I stolen your freedom away? How can you compare stealing a nut with the stealing of lives? Your Bitter Booby Prize will be being staked out beneath a nut tree and have empty shells showered down on you for the rest of your life. Don't you think I dream up some smashing Bitter Booby Prizes?'

'And he boasts about it,' murmured the shocked tortoise.

'Oh, anxious for your quiz question, eh?' mocked the varmint, his gorgeous eyes now fixed firmly on the defiant drum. 'Answer me this then, "Who is the most interesting and eloquent speaker in the whole of Africa?" Think carefully now, for you're bound to be wrong.'

'I'm the most interesting and eloquent speaker in the whole of Africa,' replied the tortoise, determined to go to his death with the truth on his beaky lips. 'And if I ever get out of this stew I'll prove it with words, not deeds.'

'Wrong, wrong, wrong, wrong,' crowed the varmint, his narrow shoulders heaving with laughter. 'I'm the most interesting and eloquent speaker in the whole of Africa. Aren't the lot of you hanging on to my every word? And talking about stews, your Bitter Booby Prize will be to be turned upside-down until you go squishy in the heat. Then I'll gobble you down for a hotpot.'

'I'll be a noble hotpot,' shouted the tortoise, proudly. 'You'll hear no begging-bowl pleas for mercy from me.'

'Isn't there a chink of compassionate light in your soul?' shouted Tumf in a way that would have delighted his chief aunt. 'How can you torture this band of brothers for answering fixed quiz questions wrong? I demand that you let us go at once, and unharmed.'

'And I demand that you stop mentioning chinks of light,' yelled the varmint, beginning to weep again. 'You know how bad it makes me feel. But all right, you demand to go free? If you get the correct answer to this question, I'll award you all the Top Bonus Prize. Are you ready for the general, and hardest question of all?'

'Get on with it, varmint,' said the brothers, wearily. 'And after we've got the answer wrong we'll prepare to fight for our lives against your Bitter Booby Prizes.'

'Here it comes then,' said the varmint, trying to stifle his giggles. 'Who do you love best of all in the world?'

'Not you, that's a fact,' cried the little elephant, scrambling painfully to his feet and sadly remembering how he used to be asked this question.

'What do you say?'

'I say we fight this unfair quizmaster,' shouted the tiny monkey, 'as I hate him the most in the world.'

'I detest him,' said the veagle, bluntly.

'And so do I,' raged the tortoise.

'Five times wrong,' whooped the varmint, triumphantly. 'The one you love best in all the word has to be me. You think I'm cuddly and beautiful, and you want to live with me in my swamp forever – don't deny it – which is why

I'm going to cancel your Bitter Booby Prizes and give you all another prize instead.'

'You mean you are going to award us all the Top Bonus Prize?' asked Tumf, his heart in his mouth as he prayed.

'Much better than that,' beamed the varmint. 'I'm going to award you all the Double-Top Bonus Prize, which is a holiday in my swamp with me for the rest of your days.'

'Never,' trumpeted the little elephant. 'We'd rather be tortured.'

'We echo Tumf,' shouted the three brothers, shuddering at the thought.

'I don't like travellers who aren't nice,' muttered the varmint, his lovely green eyes narrowing to vengeful slits. It was then that his true evil shone through his jovial quizmaster mask. 'And when travellers aren't nice, I'm not so nice.'

'But I am,' sang a voice from the oppressive gloom. 'I'm so nice that sometimes I try to hate myself for being so nice. But it never works. How can I hate my own niceness?'

The brothers peered in the direction of the voice. The varmint also stared suspiciously until suddenly his bucktoothed mouth was gaping open in amazement as out of the murky night floated an apparition. At first it appeared as a blue haze, then blossomed into a lovely blue glow, looking exactly like a chink of blue sky. The brothers basked in a blue warmth as the pink and green snake, holding his luminous tail proudly aloft, came coasting in against the island prison. He was the nicest and most welcome sight they could have wished for.

The varmint was completely bowled over. He was bouncing up and down in his broth of sludge, pointing excitedly. 'I know you,' he yelled. 'You are that bit of blue sky I once glimpsed in my youth before everything went black. Why did you go away? But never mind, you've come back to me now and I'm willing to bet that you're here to stay and brighten my life for evermore. Think carefully before you challenge my bet, for even nice bits of blue sky can win Bitter Booby Prizes for getting their answers wrong.'

The nice little snake was looking both puzzled and pleased. For a long while he alternately smiled and frowned as he looked at the trapped brothers and then at the expectant varmint.

'Please, nice little snake,' the tortoise implored. 'You once insisted on joining our band of brothers. Well, your wish is granted. Are you ready to make a great sacrifice to help our Tumf reach his new drum? Will you become the light of the varmint's life, and persuade him to release us unharmed? Please be nice.'

'At last someone appreciates and needs me. I'll gladly settle down to a nice new life in this nice swamp. I'm sure that me and the nice varmint will share a long partnership together. While he's constantly praising my astonishing tail, I will be constantly praising his good taste. It's the perfect arrangement. I'm sure we'll get on very nicely together.'

At this, the varmint whooped with joy. Throwing back his head, his whiskers and buckteeth and big belly quivering with emotion, he began to sing his heart free from the gloom and loneliness he had endured for so long as he warbled 'Blue Skies'.

'A few private words if you please, partner,' interrupted the snake, politely. At once he and the varmint went into a coloured huddle. What with the silver fur and emerald eyes of the varmint, plus the pink and green and luminous blue of the snake, the brothers sat admiring the rainbow. A rainbow of hope?

'Who's in luck then? Haven't you all done well?' cried the varmint, splashing around in the mud to face them. 'I'm pleased to announce that you've all won the Top Bonus Prize. Isn't that right, light of my life?'

'It is, and we hope that the band of brothers thoroughly enjoy their presents,' said the nice snake, beaming.

'Unless they'd like to come back next week and try to double 'em,' said the varmint, his green eyes glinting. 'Harder quiz questions of course, but much better prizes. It's up to them.'

'We'll settle for the prizes we've won today,' said Tumf, quickly, his friends vigorously nodding their agreement. 'We think that winning our freedom once is much better than trying to win it twice.'

'Then follow me and my sky-blue partner,' cried the happy varmint, slipping away through the slimy water. 'And be careful where you place your feet. My pals, the poisonous water-scorpions and the nipping crabs, get very annoyed if clumsy travellers try to squash them flat.'

Thinking all kinds of horrible thoughts, the little elephant limped down from the island refuge and began to wade in the wake of the varmint, his fearful eyes fixed firmly on the comforting glow of the snake's tail. Terrible pain shot through his bitten foot each time he was forced to put weight on it. But they were on their way out of the hateful swamp and that was all he cared about. Cold and wet and clinging to his friend's back, the cheeky monkey looked petrified as he scanned the brushing mangrove branches for slithering, stinging things. Loyal as ever, the tortoise took up a paddling station behind the stumbling Tumf, his beaky face screwed up in distaste as he floated past unspeakable objects who glared and muttered threateningly. The veagle had wisely decided to fly out of the swamp to await them in the foothills of the bendy mountains, but only on his third desperate attempt did he manage to become airborne. Every twist and turn through the swamp held fresh terrors for the other three. Just as the exhausted little elephant was about to give up and die in his tracks for the third time, there was a jubilant cry.

'I see a chink of light ahead,' shouted the monkey. 'Tumf, at last we're emerging from night into day.'

Tumf gazed through bleary eyes at the way ahead. The monkey was right.

'Behold your Top Bonus Prize,' cried the varmint. 'Run and claim it before I change my mind and dish out Bitter Booby Prizes instead.'

'Good luck, and safe travelling,' called the

nice snake from the edge of the swamp. 'May you all find your niche in life as I've found mine. May your lights never shine under a bushel – mine certainly won't.'

So saying, the odd couple vanished into the gloom of the mangrove swamp.

8
Going Round the Bend

'Round the bend and round again
Till your heart breaks once again . . .'

It was sad to see the weary and dejected friends drumming and singing on the slope of the mountains as they prepared to tackle the next stage of their journey through the song. How many more cruel blows could they take? Not even the splendid sight of the green-sided, snow-capped mountains boosted their spirits. Not even the enthusiastic veagle could spark their interest in the climb. Slowly and painfully, the little elephant began the long and winding upward plod to the pass through the snowy peaks. The veagle was too worried about Tumf to fly ahead. Instead, he hopped and fluttered in the lead, casting worried glances over his bony shoulder. It was plain that Tumf's limp was getting worse. He could manage only a three-legged shuffle. The monkey had slid from Tumf's back to clasp the tip of Tumf's trunk in his paw. Trying with all of his heart and strength, he tugged and willed the little elephant onwards. Each time Tumf gave a brave smile, the monkey grinned back with relief. Each time Tumf winced in pain, the monkey grimaced in sympathy. The tortoise no longer needed to sprint to keep up with Tumf and grieved unobserved. He ambled along behind and from close-to he was able to see the blood dripping from that swollen foot. No one spoke.

It was the final bend before the summit that proved to be the ultimate test of courage. They had barely trudged around it before a boulder came rolling down. It missed the dodging veagle by centimetres. If it was meant to be a warning shot across their bows, the hail of missiles that followed wasn't. They were under intense fire. Ignoring the cries of protest from his friends Tumf limped forward to take the full force of the barrage. He did not flinch as the sharp-edged stones thudded into his flesh.

'It must be an avalanche, an act of God,' yelled the veagle, fluttering to take cover inside a flimsy bush on the side of the trail. 'Turn and run back round the bend, Tumf. Do you want to be killed?'

'It's no act of God,' cried the terrified monkey, sheltering behind Tumf's huge foot. 'That's my dad raining down rocks on us. He's mad enough to tip the whole mountain down on our heads to get at me. I wish I was a hero like Tumf, I'd march up this bend and accept the thrashing of my life to save my friends. Someone will have to order me to march into my dad's jaws of death.'

'The only order you'll receive is to run for cover when I tell you,' shouted Tumf, stifling a cry of pain as a brickbat caught him flush on the end of his trunk. He waited for a lull in the attack, then yelled: 'Now, little friend, dash over and join the veagle in the bush while I act as a barricade. Now!'

In a flash the monkey was up and scampering. Inside two seconds he was thankfully squeezing into the bird's hideout. Inside another two seconds he was coughing and complaining about the veagle's moulting feathers that were making him suffocate.

'Hard pounding, young friend,' came the tortoise's muffled voice. He had advanced from the rear to take up a new station beside Tumf's front foot. His tender parts were tucked away in his shell, hence his muffled voice. He was confident that his hard back could resist most of the artillery but he dreaded the whistle that would herald the arrival of the 'big one'. 'Someone up there didn't wish me to speak,' he yelled to Tumf. 'It's me they're after. Save yourself, my friend. As for me, I'm going to advance up this bend and give something or someone a piece of my mind. Goodbye, little elephant, I'm going to march towards the sound of the guns.'

'Oh no you're not,' Tumf shouted. With a sweep of his large front foot he sent the surprised tortoise spinning tip over top in the direction of the scrawny bush where the veagle and the monkey cowered. Soon the fragile plant was tossing and creaking as the three brothers jostled for space and argued bitterly over who loved Tumf best. In the meantime the little elephant staggered to a halt at the top of the path to confront his persecutors. And what an ungodly-looking crew they were.

Baboons squatted in a rough semicircle, with rock-filled paws raised menacingly as the little elephant, with his wounded hide running blood, approached them. The baboons were jealously guarding the pass through the mountains behind them. The pass shone with light and promised paradise. Tumf glanced round curiously and noticed stone-covered mounds that dotted the plateau. A large baboon suddenly sprang forward to challenge Tumf, his yellow teeth bared in a snarl.

'Go on, I dare you,' he barked, leaping on to a high rock to look Tumf in the eye. 'Make a dash for the pass and see how far you get. Many have tried, and you can see what happened to them.' He pointed at the mounds. 'But if you want to make a stab at it, come on little suck-pap elephant and make my day.'

'The mounds are graves, then?' said Tumf, trembling.

'We've always believed in giving our victims a proper burial,' mocked the baboon to a chorus of cheers and hoots from his troupe. 'We'd have liked to lay 'em out in neat rows with flowers on top, but we never found the time. Never mind, our victims aren't worrying, being pretty well stone-cold dead, and you will be too if you try to break through our cordon. Do try, we haven't had a good burial in ages.'

'You mean "burials", dad,' sniggered a small

baboon who had leapt on to the rock. 'There's always the chance that the cowards he calls friends will conquer their fear and join him here.'

'Four fresh graves we'll dig today,' intoned the cordon of hopeful baboons. 'For the pass will not be passed.'

'Never again will travellers insult us,' cried the little baboon, angrily clashing two stones together. 'Never again will they smarm us with compliments, only to change their minds when they reach safety.'

'But why should you wish to kill me and my friends?' stammered Tumf, confused. 'We've done you no harm. We only want to travel through the pass in peace.'

'They all say that,' shouted the large baboon, glaring his hatred. 'As soon as they were through they'd shout nasty things, and tell us what they really thought. So now nobody gets through the pass that we guard day and night.'

'But we brothers wouldn't dream of insulting you once we'd passed through,' protested Tumf, sincerely. 'What kind of nasty remarks are you talking about?'

'They said how sweetly we baboons smelled,' raged the large one. 'But as soon as they were safe on the other side they would hold their noses and jeer that we stunk like skunks. Others would say how gentle and kind we were, but once through the pass they called us uncouth bullies. But the final straw was when a party arrived and commented on how clean we kept ourselves and then accused us of being absolutely crawling with fleas, which was a terrible lie; we baboons spend most of our time picking out each other's fleas.'

'That was the last nail in the coffin of all future travellers, eh Dad?' cried the small baboon. 'It was then that your patience snapped and you passed the law ordering all travellers to be stoned and buried.'

'It certainly was, son,' said the large baboon, shaking with anger. 'If I hadn't passed that law the whole of our troupe would have gone round the bend with frustration. I did the right thing, didn't I?' A roar of approval greeted his words, followed by a mighty clashing of rocks.

'Well, I can assure you that me and my band of brothers would never insult you,' said Tumf, vehemently. 'And when my friends arrive, you'll find that we say nice things and really mean them. I can sincerely vouch that you won't want to stone and bury us when you find out what we're really like.'

At that moment the veagle and the tortoise and the cheeky monkey came toiling on to the plateau. Seeing the troupe of baboons and the rocks in their paws, the impetuous bird prepared to give them a piece of his mind, with strong backing from the tortoise.

'So, you lot are responsible for the rock-throwing, eh?' bellowed the bird, eyeing the large baboon, the tortoise eyeing the smaller one.

'Veagle, tortoise,' hissed Tumf, frantically. 'If we could have a few words in private before you say any more.'

'Phew, what a stink,' shouted the monkey, neatly putting his paw in it.

'Be quiet, cheeky monkey,' pleaded Tumf. 'You don't know what you're saying.'

But the monkey was in full flow. He continued, his cheeky gaze taking in the now silent troupe of baboons, 'So these are the uncouth bullies who tried to kill us?'

'Please, monkey, you are on the way to ruining everything,' groaned the little elephant.

But the monkey ignored him. He knew what he was doing. Being a monkey, he knew a lot about baboons. He continued to bait the quiet semicircle of watchers. 'So, who's got the most fleas amongst you lot? But then, I expect you've all got so many they're impossible to count.'

'We're all dead,' wept Tumf to the shell-shocked veagle and the tortoise. 'The cheeky monkey has as good as put us in our graves already. And I was just about to plead our case, too. Now we'll never get through the pass to complete our journey through the song. Do you see those mounds, my dear friends? Well, very soon there'll be four more.'

'You mean those mounds are graves?' said the horrified bird.

'Of past travellers,' said Tumf, nodding his sad head.

'But we are travellers,' said the tortoise, dumbly. 'Do you mean to say . . . ?'

The little elephant bowed his head.

But the cheeky monkey sat looking the large and small baboons in the eye. His sheer brazenness was awesome. Then all at once the big baboon spoke.

'Are you saying that we baboons not only smell, but we are also uncouth bullies?' he said to the monkey, his eyes sad. 'And you also reckon we have fleas?'

'That is correct,' replied the monkey, briskly.

'And you won't change that opinion?' said the large baboon, a sob in his voice.

'That all depends,' said the monkey, carefully. 'If me and my friends are allowed to leave without fear of more rocks landing on our heads, I'd certainly consider it.'

'If we let you through the pass, what would you shout when you were safely on the other side?' questioned the large baboon.

'Something completely different, probably,' said the monkey. 'So are you going to let us go, and take a chance on what we shout?'

The large baboon and the little baboon turned to face the silent troupe ranged on the rocks before the shining pass. At once a mighty roar sounded around the plateau as the baboons indicated that they were prepared to take the gamble. Then they leapt from their perches to clear the way for the band of brothers.

'I don't understand,' whispered Tumf as he limped through the pass.

'Neither do I, but just keep going,' hissed the veagle.

'I don't believe this,' muttered the tortoise. 'I'm still waiting for that extra-large, shell-crushing rock to come whistling over.'

But it didn't, and sloping gently down before them were a series of undulating fields strewn with flowers and crisscrossed by tinkling streams. It seemed like paradise.

'Stop and look back, everyone,' ordered the monkey on Tumf's back. 'We have a favour to return.'

All three gazed back at the gap in the mountains. Clustered around it were the baboon troupe, totally silent, their muzzly faces looking expectant.

'On behalf of this band of brothers I would like to send a message from our hearts,' called the cheeky monkey. 'We believe that baboons not only smell like roses, are not only sweet and gentle, but also they don't even possess one flea between them.'

At his kind words the baboons began to

whoop and cheer and bounce up and down
with joy. The debt had been repaid, and now
everyone could be happy.

'I still don't understand,' said the little
elephant, confused. His limp was now less
pronounced as he lumbered through a lush
field, his enormous feet crushing acres of
daisies. 'After the way the monkey insulted the
baboons we should all be lying beneath

mounds with no flowers on top. So why did they let us through the pass, little monkey? Why were you so confident that they would?'

'One has to understand the baboon mind,' grinned the monkey. 'All past travellers praised the baboons while on the dangerous side of the pass. But the baboons wanted praise from this safe side when the travellers could afford to speak the truth.'

'Were you sincere?' questioned the little elephant, pausing in mid-step as a mischievous mouse dashed by. 'Your compliments sounded a bit over the top to me.'

'They heard what they wanted to hear,' shrugged the monkey. 'Who am I to deny even a vicious troupe of baboons a snatch of happiness.'

'Murderers aren't entitled to be happy,' scowled the tortoise. 'When my day comes I'll alert Africa to the killers amongst us in a speech entitled: "Why should our Fellow Africans be buried beneath Flowerless Mounds just because Baboons can't face being Odious?" That should stop the baboons' fetish for digging graves.'

'Personally, I'm not at all interested in the mind of the baboon,' said the veagle, impatiently. 'I've got work to do. You do know that we're now on the last lap of the journey through the aunts' song? But there's still some scouting to be done. Many a quest foundered because the travellers thought they were home and dry. We still have to cross that thick jungle beyond. And there's something else you might not have realised . . .'

'What something else?' said the tortoise, indignantly. 'There's nothing I can't realise, being a deep thinker.'

'Oh no?' the veagle interrupted. 'Let's pause in this meadow and sing Tumf's song from the beginning, then you'll realise something. Come on, this is very important. Are you ready?'

Reluctantly the tortoise began to drum a tumf-ti-tumf-tumf beat on his shell. Miffed, and wondering what all the fuss was about, Tumf and the cheeky monkey began to sing the song of the wise aunts from top to bottom:

'Through the jungle, across the plain
Into the desert and out again
Into the river and out again
Through the swamp and out again
Round the bend and round again
Till your heart breaks once again
Then . . .'

'Stop,' cried the veagle.

'But we haven't finished the song yet,' said Tumf, surprised.

'It's finished as far as directions are concerned,' said the bird. 'It doesn't mention where we're supposed to go from here. All it says is that Tumf should sniff through his trunk and flap back his ear and listen for the tumf-ti-tumf beat of a drum. But the song doesn't say where we should be when we listen for it.'

'So we've come to a dead end, veagle,' said the worried little elephant. 'Now what do we do?'

'Well, we shouldn't pin our hopes on the veagle, for a start,' said the tortoise, his eyes twinkling. 'I've already said that our bird will prove less than useless up a dead end. I say we camp here and wait until something turns up, like some vital clue that will come from the blue.'

'I say we should keep moving,' said the monkey, uneasily. 'If my dad is still hot on my heels I'd sooner be a moving target than a still one.'

'So what's the answer?' Tumf appealed. He was standing as tall as he could on the balls of his huge feet, his trunk upraised and sniffing, his wide ears flapping to catch the faintest strains of a distant drum. But he heard nothing.

'Well, I'm going to scout these meadows and the jungle beyond,' said the veagle impatiently. 'Hanging around waiting for something to happen will get us nowhere.'

'A great idea,' shouted Tumf as the bird wobbled into the air. 'In the meantime the rest of us will snatch a bite to eat and enjoy a nap amongst the daisies before we plod down to join you. I expect that you'll have solved all our problems by the time we get there.'

'Let's hope we don't find him up a dead end with his beak crushed to one side,' prayed the tortoise.

'And up that dead end will be my dad,' worried the monkey. 'He could take the veagle hostage in return for me. Would you turn me in for the safe return of the veagle?'

'Let's be optimistic and relax for a while,' urged Tumf. 'There's nothing we can do for the moment. And I don't know about you, but I'm famished.'

A few minutes later the little elephant was tearing leafy fronds from the surrounding bushes and cramming them down his hungry throat. The monkey had scampered off in search of a nut tree. He found a lone one with three branches, each limb bearing a single nut. Cautiously nibbling two, he was just about to snatch for the third when his nervously flicking eyes detected a flurry of furious movement behind a clump of sunflowers. Babbling in fear, he bolted back to leap on to the broad shoulders of the little elephant. Meanwhile, the tortoise had sprinted down to the stream. He was delighted to see that its banks were awash with his favourite kind of organic, green grub. And so, after a good meal and several draughts of cold water each, the three brothers left that delicious meadow to continue their downward journey, a spring in their heels and hope in their hearts as they approached the edge of the thick, steaming jungle. Again and again the hopeful little elephant paused to sniff through his trunk, to flap back his ears to catch the sound of a drum. But all he could hear was the clicking of grasshoppers, the noisy quarrelling of parrots, and the sigh of the wind through the long grasses.

9

A New Drum for a New Day

The veagle hadn't so much landed as crashed. Picking himself up he stared gloomily at the two tail-feathers fluttering in the breeze. At this rate he wouldn't have a feather to his name, and who would believe that he was a veagle? He was quickly shaken from his self-pitying mood when he heard, sounding nearer and nearer, the hysterical trumpeting of a young elephant. Then all at once the bird was shocked to see Tumf charging towards him, the monkey clinging grimly to his neck, the tortoise sprinting alongside. Behind them bounded four lions in hot pursuit, their tawny coats glowing golden in the sunshine. It seemed touch-and-go whether the little elephant and his friends could gain the safety of the jungle before they were cuffed to the ground and devoured.

The veagle was filled with a terrible rage. His take-off was perfect as he flew into battle. Never before had he felt and looked more like an eagle as he levelled into a low glide and dashed himself into the faces of the surprised

lions. Swooping and diving and screaming his anger, he diverted their attention long enough for his friends to escape. Robbed of their dinner, the frustrated lions skidded to a halt. After a few sniffing prowls up and down the jungle edge, plus some frustrated roars and swats at the air, they returned to the grassy meadows, the veagle dive-bombing their heads every lope of the way. Bursting with pride the bird fluttered back to where his friends lay wheezing and trembling in the bushes.

'How many more dangers must we face,' wept the little elephant, sorry for himself and his friends. 'This time, I beg you, let me lie here and die, I can't be brave any more. I have failed.'

'Did you pick up a clue as to what we do next?' asked the anxious tortoise. 'If you didn't, Tumf's journey ends right here. He's been so strong until now.'

'And here comes another danger,' yelled the monkey, pointing, 'and it's even more dangerous than charging lions.'

A solitary, mischievous mouse suddenly darted towards the tip of Tumf's exhausted trunk. But before the brothers could rush forward, the mouse placed a sweet-smelling, reviving herb for Tumf to sniff at before scurrying away. It seemed even prankster mice loved small elephants in trouble.

Suddenly, from deep inside the jungle, they heard the tumf-ti-tumf-tumf of a drum. Instantly, all their aches and pains vanished. They had not failed after all. The little elephant was whooping for joy as he struggled to rise. Scarred, but no longer bowed, he turned his over-large head towards the depths of the jungle to hear that lovely sound again. Silence, and more silence threatened to dash his hopes.

'Perhaps we only imagined it,' said the monkey, hesitantly. 'But I could swear I heard a drum.'

'Well, I heard the tumf-ti-tumf-tumf of a drum,' said the tortoise, stoutly. 'As a drummer myself, I should know what a drum sounds like.'

'Then why has it stopped?' cried Tumf.

'What if we imagined it? What if it was just a heavy downpour of rain drumming on the banana leaves deep in the jungle? Now what do we do, veagle? I can't think any more.'

'We finish the song, of course,' said the bird. 'We must sing the song to the very end, and pray that that is the right way. So are you all ready to drum and sing?'

'We are,' shouted the others. 'Let's finish the song and pray that the last word and note doesn't fade into silence.' So they sang so enthusiastically that they attracted an audience of mice and anteaters and other swinging, creeping creatures who all sang along lustily when the beat of the tortoise entered their souls:

' . . .Then . . .
Sniff through your trunk and flap back your ear
Now can you hear it ever so clear . . .?
Quicken your step and you'll safely come
To the tumf-ti-tumf-tumf of a drum . . .'

To the loud cheers of the growing choir, the little elephant got the message. Standing tall, his scarred hide quivering with anticipation, he began to sniff energetically through his trunk, his sail-like ears flapping for all they were worth. And suddenly the sound of a drum came as clear as crystal, and he smelled an old, familiar scent. With a trumpet of gladness he lumbered headlong through the jungle, his friends and lots of hangers-on following hard on his heels. The hypnotic beat of the drum reached a crescendo as he dug his front feet into the red earth to slow down. As Tumf timidly entered the clearing the drumming stopped. For one brief moment his mind flashed back to a time so long ago and far away. It was as if he was returning from a bathe in his beloved lake.

The elephant herd stood smiling, their trunks swaying in a warm welcome as Tumf shyly advanced, his own trunk tucked into his mouth for comfort. The circle of young and old aunts opened up. There in the centre of the clearing squatted a small elephant of Tumf's age, her trunk poised over the hollow log-drum. Her squinty blue eyes danced with mischief as she appraised Tumffington.

'Welcome, little orphaned Tumffington from over the mountains,' said a large, wrinkled lady. She looked and sounded like a chief aunt. 'Our grapevine of drums informed us that you were making a bid to join us.'

'And here I am, chief aunt,' said the squirming Tumf, hoping that he lived up to her expectations.

'We've prayed long and hard that the song of your dead family would guide you safely here,' said the aunt, her eyes misting over. 'Now our task is to mend your broken heart and to teach

you a new and happier song. Be one with us, as we are one with you. Be happy here, and make us happy too. This is your new home, Tumffington. Live and grow amongst us, for we need the young to cherish as our numbers dwindle.'

'Thank you, chief aunt,' wept Tumf, his fears and anxieties melting away. 'I'll try to be as good as gold and make you proud of me.'

'We know you are very brave, otherwise you would never have found us. Chief aunt would have been proud of you.' Before Tumf could feel sad, the small drummer giggled.

'Tumffington. What a silly name. But he's welcome to play on my drum, even if his name is silly.'

'Only my full name is silly,' flared Tumf, his confidence growing as the younger aunts plied him with bananas and leafy fronds. 'Amongst my friends I'm known as Tumf, and that isn't a silly name.'

'Oh, so you haven't forgotten us then?' yelled the tortoise from the edge of the clearing. 'You do still remember your band of brothers who stuck by you through thick and thin? For a moment we feared that all the fuss and bananas were going to your head. So when are you going to introduce us to your new family?'

'Tiffington, dear,' ordered the chief aunt, frowning at her niece. 'Leave that drum alone and welcome Tumffington's band of brothers into our clearing. The least we can do is to thank them for their efforts on his behalf.'

'That's an even sillier name than mine,' chortled Tumf, beginning to feel very much at home amongst his new family. 'Do as you're told, Tiffington.'

'I'd better warn you that my nickname is Tiff, because when I fly off the handle everyone knows about it. I'm an expert at having tiffs with young orphans from over the mountains, who couldn't play a drum to save their lives.'

Tumf floundered for a smart answer. Open-mouthed and speechless he watched as she rose from her drum and sauntered across to Tumf's impatient friends. Her eyes glinted with mischief again as she spoke. 'Welcome, tatty old vulture, welcome gabby tortoise, welcome, cheeky monkey,' she said in a charming voice. 'My chief aunt says for me to welcome you into our clearing. I expect she wants to shower you with praise for sticking by silly Tumffington through thick and thin. Well, don't expect me to hail you as saints, for I can't abide folk with halos round their heads. But I certainly admire your guts and determination to deliver my silly cousin to his new home. So come on in, unless you'd rather stay where you are and have a bawl-out tiff with me?'

Smarting from her jokey welcome, Tumf's loyal friends moved into the clearing.

'These are my lovely friends, chief aunt,' said Tumf, proudly. 'If it wasn't for them I'd have died many times along the way.'

'We owe a debt to your friends for bringing you safe to us,' said the chief aunt. She smiled down at the balding veagle, the shell-cratered tortoise, the frightened and tousled monkey, who were gazing anxiously up at her.

'Couldn't you give them a reward, chief aunt?' begged Tumf.

'If it's in our power, we certainly will,' the chief aunt replied. She looked down at the veagle, her wise eyes soft. 'And what do you desire from life, poor bird?'

The veagle's eyes filled with hope as he began to stammer. 'If you please, chief aunt, I yearn to be accepted for what I feel I am. I know I'm only a baldy old vulture, but I have the heart of an eagle. I just wish to spend the rest of my days soaring through the snowy mountains, respected by all.'

'And what about you, tortoise?' questioned the aunt, noting with sympathy his rock-scarred shell. 'What does our knight in battered armour wish from life?'

'My wish is to give not to receive,' cried the tortoise, addressing the chief aunt as if she were a public meeting. 'I stand here to bring to your attention the sorry state of our beloved Africa. I believe that if I could roam over our land speaking to vast audiences that together we could put right the evils that plague our society. Under my leadership we'd soon put a stop to the shooting of elephants for their tusks and our furry friends for their posh coats: that's what I wish to give to life, chief aunt.'

'And how about cheeky-face?' the large lady smiled. With the tip of her trunk she reached out to soothe the agitated little nut-thief. 'What do you want above all?'

'Believe me, chief aunt,' the monkey sobbed. 'I just want to become known as the most honest monkey in Africa. When I swing through the trees I want folk to say, "There goes a monkey who wouldn't steal an extra nut from anyone." Then perhaps my dad would stop chasing me to thrash me within an inch of my life. Also, perhaps, my mum would get down off the fence and give me an affectionate hug. Oh, if only I could be forgiven for my past crimes, lovely lady.'

'Well, chief aunt?' appealed Tumf, his trunk tucked into his mouth again as he anxiously waited for the verdict. 'Can you help my friends to find the happiness that I have found?'

'Their happiness lies in different directions,' sighed the chief aunt. 'It might even lie back where they started from.'

'Do you mean that my brothers must face more terrible wanderings across Africa to find a bit of peace of mind?' said Tumf, aghast. 'But that isn't fair after they've suffered so much already.'

'The road to happiness and contentment is never easy,' replied the sad old lady. 'We can only wish them well and send them on their lonely way with a prayer.'

'And a song, chief aunt,' cried Tiffy Tiffington, spiritedly. 'A song brought silly Tumffington to us, why can't a song guide his friends along *their* lonely roads? Come on, Tumf, let's prepare to drum while our aunts think up some encouraging words to sing along.'

'Our Tiffington grows kinder and wiser,' said the delighted chief aunt. She spoke to her sisters who immediately began to hum.

Meanwhile, the two young elephants settled

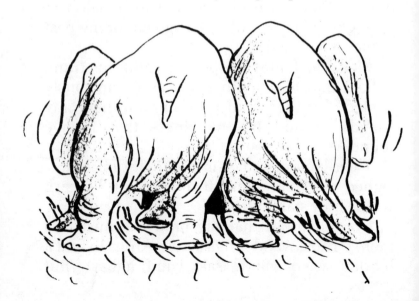

side by side by their hollow log, trunks poised to make music. But soon tears were flowing from their squinty grey eyes as they watched the bald veagle and the dented tortoise and the nervous, cheeky monkey line up in the clearing, their heads held high ready to march off in search of their hearts' desires.

Tumf-ti-tumf-tumf went the beat of the drum. Then suddenly the choir of aunts began to sing a song filled with love and sadness. But elephant aunts never tell lies which is why their song contained little hope until the very end:

'Into the heartbreak and out again
Snatching at hope and dashed again
Rivers and plains that nourish our land
Please do not savage our gallant band.
Into sweet dreams and out again
Into the nightmare and out again . . .
Then . . .
Sniff the fresh wind and listen intent
There goes all misery . . .up and went . . .
Home are the brothers, their hearts glad and free . . .
Yearning and longing for thee . . .'

To the sound of music Tumf's loyal band of brothers marched out of the clearing to go their separate ways to happiness.

'Goodbye and good luck, my friends,' wept Tumf. 'Let's hope we'll meet again one day to sing a happier song. How I wish I could go with you and share the dangers, but . . .'

'Never wish that, Tumf my love,' cried the veagle. 'Your journey is over. Our journey would only be a backward step for you. Don't worry, I'm sure that we will all find our own heaven one fine day. Just keep beating your drum and praying for us. As elephants, I know you'll never forget us. When I'm soaring through my frozen mountains, accepted and respected by the king of birds himself, it will be such a comfort to know that you still think of me.'

'And when I've stamped my mark on Africa I'll be listening, too,' shouted the tortoise. 'On the other hand, if you'd rather visit me in person, don't worry about me being too famous and stuck-up to enjoy a chinwag with an old friend. Just force your way past my bodyguard and shout that you demand to see the tortoise in charge. You'll find me eager to spare a few moments to chat about the old times.'

'And if I ever meet my Tumf again he'll find me as honest as the day is long,' vowed the tiny nut-thief. 'I'll proudly introduce him to my mum and dad as the most honest elephant in Africa come to visit the most honest monkey in Africa. Honest, Tumf, I really mean to change my ways for the better if I ever get back home.'

Their voices died away, swallowed by the

thick greenery of the jungle. Time alone would tell whether the hopes and dreams of Tumf's band of brothers would come true. Maybe, thanks to them, a drum will sound out across Africa and herald a new dawn for a happy and healed land where elephants and all creatures are safe.